"ATOMIC CONVERTER FOUR HAS BLOWN!"

The men at the mammoth atomic plant in Kimberly knew what that meant, but they didn't have time to think about it.

The new process had run wild, and the only man who knew how to control its deadly potential was trapped inside a swirling chaos of radioactive materials . . .

Dozens were already dead, more were dying, and only an impossible operation could save the day.

If the berserk nuclear reaction couldn't be stopped, within hours half of North America would be totally destroyed!

Rave Reviews
For A Frightening Look
Into Our Future

"Leaders of Congress and industry are currently debating the catastrophe potential of commercial atomic plants and the amount of Federal indemnity that should be set therefore. It's a pity these well-intentioned gropers in the dark don't take time out to read this masterpiece of realistic description of what could happen when a nuclear reactor takes the bit in its teeth . . . a war of nerves with a power pile bubbling toward a blowup!"

—The Sunday New York Times

"A wholly admirable blend of prophetic thinking, warm human values, and powerful narrative suspense, this is strongly commended."

—Anthony Boucher

nerves

by
lester del rey

ballantine books · new york

A shorter version of this novel apeared in *Astounding Stories*,
© 1942 by Street & Smith Publications, Inc. Renewed 1970 by
The Condé Nast Publications, Inc.

Library of Congress Catalog Card Number: 56-9579

ISBN 0-345-24995-X-150

Manufactured in the United States of America

First Revised Edition:
First Printing: April, 1976

First Edition: June, 1956
Fifth Printing: February, 1974

Cover art by Don Brautigan

TO FREDERIK POHL

for insistence, persistence,
assistance—and existence!

nerves

chapter 1

THE JANGLING of the telephone gnawed at Doc Ferrel's sleep. His efforts to cut it off by burying his head deeper in the pillow only made him more aware of it. Across the room, he heard Emma stirring uneasily. He could just make out her body under the sheets by the dim light of the early morning.

Nobody had any business calling at that hour!

Resentment cut through the last mists of sleep. He groped to his feet and fumbled for his robe. When a man nears sixty, with gray hair and enlarged waistline to show for it, he should be entitled to his sleep. But the phone went on insistently. Then, as he reached the head of the stairs, he began to fear that it would stop. Reaching it just too late would be the final aggravation.

He half-stumbled down the stairs until he could reach the receiver. "Ferrel speaking."

Relief and fatigue were mixed in the voice at the other end. "This is Palmer, Doc. Did I wake you up?"

"I was just sitting down to supper," Ferrel told him bitterly. Palmer was the manager of the atomics plant where Doc worked, and at least nominally his boss. "What's the matter? Your grandson got a stomach-ache, or has the plant finally blown up? And what's it to me at this hour? Anyhow, I thought you said I could forget about the plant today."

Palmer sighed faintly, as if he'd expected Doc's

| I |

reaction and had been bracing himself for it. "I know. That's what I called about. Of course, if you've made plans you can't break, I can't ask you to change them. God knows, you've earned a day off. But . . ."

He left it hanging. Ferrel knew it was bait. If he showed any interest now, he was hooked. He waited, and finally Palmer sighed again.

"Okay, Doc. I guess I had no business bothering you. It's just that I don't trust Dr. Blake's tact. But maybe I can convince him that smart cracks don't go over well with a junket of visiting congressmen. Go back to sleep. Sorry I woke you up."

"Wait a minute," Ferrel said quickly. He shook his head, wishing he'd had at least a swallow of coffee to clear his brain. "I thought the investigating committee was due next week."

Palmer, like a good angler, gave him a second's grace before he set the hook.

"They were, but I got word the plans are changed. They'll be here, complete with experts and reporters, sometime this forenoon. And with that bill up before Congress . . . Well, have a good day, Doc."

Ferrel swore to himself. All he had to do now was to hang up, of course. Handling the committee was Palmer's responsibility; it was his plant that would be moved to some wasteland if the cursed bill was passed. Doc's job was concerned only with the health and safety of the men. "I'll have to talk it over with Emma," he growled at last. "Where'll you be in ten minutes? Home?"

"I'm at the plant."

Doc looked at the clock. Just after six. If Palmer thought things were that serious . . . Yet it was the last day of Dick's brief visit home from medical school, and they'd been planning on this day all week! Emma had her heart set on making it a happy family affair.

A sound from the head of the stairs made him

look up. Emma was standing there in a cotton robe and worn old slippers. Without make-up and with her hair hanging loose, she looked like a little girl who had grown old overnight without quite understanding it. Her face was carefully stripped of expression; she'd learned to conceal her feelings back in the days when Ferrel had maintained a general practice. But the tautness of her throat muscles and the way she cinched the belt around her too-thin figure showed that she had heard and how she felt.

She shrugged and nodded, trying to smile at him as she started down the stairs, favoring her bad hip.

"Breakfast will take a little time," she said quietly. "Try to get some sleep. I'll wake Dick and explain it to him."

She was heading for the kitchen as he turned back to the phone. "All right, Palmer. I'll be out. Nine okay?"

"Thanks, Doc. Nine will be fine," Palmer answered. Emma was already starting coffee in the kitchen. Doc turned toward her, and then hesitated. She was right; he needed the extra sleep.

Sleep wouldn't come, though. The resiliency of youth was long gone, and now even the sound habits of his middle life seemed to be failing. Maybe Blake was right in his kidding; maybe he was growing old! He had caught himself wondering as he looked at the firm-muscled figure of his son, so like Doc's memory of himself at the same age, and so unlike what the mirror showed now.

The situation at the plant kept gnawing at his mind. He'd paid little attention to the increasing reaction on the part of the public against atomic activity. But of late he'd been forced to recognize the growing tension among the workers, caused by the sudden whipping up of the fear of atomic plants after so many years of acceptance. Now there were citizens' protest meetings, and a number of badly drawn, hasty bills were being submitted to Congress—bills that would force most atomic plants to move far from inhabited territory. But he'd put all that down to the normally noisy crackpot fringe. Still, if Palmer took it seriously, maybe he'd been wrong. Maybe things had really got worse since the breakdown of the Croton atomic plant a few months ago. It was only a minor mishap there, really. But it had resulted in a mild dose of radiation contamination over a hundred square miles or more; it seemed to be nobody's fault, but it had been a nine-day newspaper scandal, and it might have served as a focal point for all the buried superstitions and fears about atomics.

Ferrel finally gave up and began dressing, surprised at how much time had gone already. The house was filled with the smell of hot biscuits, and he realized Emma was making a production of their last meal together on their son's only vacation. He heard her waking Dick and explaining the situation while he shaved. The boy sounded a lot less disappointed over the changed plans than she did; somehow children seemed to care less than their parents about such things.

The boy was already at the table when Doc came down, poring over the pages of the early edition of the Kimberly *Republican*. He glanced up and passed over half of the paper. "Hi, Dad. Tough about today. But Mom and I decided we'd drive you to work in my car so we'll see a little more of you. I guess this anti-atom craze is getting serious, eh?"

"Palmer's worried, that's all. It's his job to be over-cautious." At the moment, Doc was more interested in the biscuits and honey.

Dick shook his head. "Better look at the editorial," he advised.

Ferrel turned to it, though he usually had no use

for the canned editorials in the Guilden papers. Then he saw that this was signed and written as the major policy of the newspaper. It concerned the bill to evacuate all plants engaged in atomic transmutation or the creation of radioactive isotopes to areas at least fifty miles from any city of over ten thousand population. Superficially, the editorial was an unbiased study of the bill, but it equated such things as the wealth the industry had built on one side with the health of children menaced by accidental release of radioactives on the other. Intellectually, it proved the plants must stay; emotionally, it said the exact opposite; and most of the readers here would think with their emotions first.

On the front page, the feature story was on a citizens' meeting for the bill. The number reported in attendance and the list of speakers was a second shock. Before National Atomics Products had been built near the city, Kimberly had been only a small town like many others in Missouri. Now it numbered nearly a hundred thousand, and depended for its prosperity almost entirely on National; there were other industries, but they were National's children. Even those which didn't depend on artificial isotopes still needed the cheap power that came almost as a by-product.

No matter what the other Guilden papers screamed, or how crazy other cities went, it was incredible to find such a reaction here.

He threw aside his paper in disgust, not even bothering with the ball scores. He glanced grumpily at the time. "I guess I'd better get going."

Emma refilled his coffee, then limped up the stairs to finish dressing. Ferrel watched her slow steps unhappily. Maybe they should have bought one of the single-story houses that were coming back in fashion. A private escalator would be even better, but Dick's education didn't leave enough for that. Maybe in another year, though, when the boy was through school . . .

"Dad." Dick's face was serious now, and his voice had dropped to hide his words from his mother. "Dad, we've been discussing this stuff at school. After all, medicine has to have some of the isotopes National makes, so it's important to all of us. And something's been bothering me. Suppose you get called up before Congress to testify on the danger?"

Ferrel hadn't thought of that. "Suppose I do?" It could happen; he was as well known as anyone else in the field. "I don't have anything to hide. It won't hurt me to give them the truth."

"If that's what they want. And if the man running it isn't after good publicity in the Guilden press." Dick started to go on indignantly, then threw a look toward the stairs and subsided. Emma was just starting down.

Doc swallowed the rest of his coffee and followed out to the boy's little turbine-powered convertible. Normally he preferred the slower but dependable bus to the plant, but he couldn't argue with Emma's wishes now. He climbed into the back, muttering to himself as the wind whipped at him. Conversation was almost impossible, between the sound of the air screaming around the sporty windshield and the muffled roar of the turbine, stripped of half its muffler to give a sound of false power. Well, maybe the girls at school who found such things attractive would outgrow it; Doc hoped so, though he had his doubts. Or maybe—he thought again—he was just growing old.

He watched the houses along the fifteen-mile road change from apartments to the endless rows of development huts that had grown up on all sides of Kimberly—prefabricated boxes with convertible rooms, set down on tiny lots that looked alike. Most of them showed evidence that the trailer had been their ancestor, and a few even had the wheels on which they'd been shipped—possibly indicating a lack of faith in the permanence of the owner's employment.

The road was jammed, and in places they slowed to a crawl. From a neighboring car, Doc heard the swearing against "ignorant Hoosiers" that was still almost a trademark of some Missourians. A horn blasted out and another driver yelled, "Get off the road, you damned atomjerks! We don't want you here!"

Atomjerks! Three years ago, being an atomjack was almost enough to insure good credit and respect. Times, it seemed, had changed.

There were other significant changes as they began to near the plant. More and more *Vacant* signs were in front of houses. Once there had been a premium on locations along the highway near the plant. But now the fear for the safety of the families of the workers was apparently stronger than the desire for easy commuting. Obviously, even many of those most closely associated with National were not immune to the growing unease.

He was almost relieved when they swung off the main road onto the private highway that led to the front gates. The sprawling, haphazard cluster of utilitarian buildings, offices and converter-housings covered acres of ground and was set back nearly a mile from the turnpike. Here the land was deserted, cared for by the ground crews who kept down the weeds. Laws had already forced a safety zone around the plants, though it had been no great hardship to National. Behind the plant lay a great tract of barren land, stretching back down a brackish little stream to a swamp farther away. That, at least, was useful, since it served as a dumping ground for their non-radioactive wastes. Even the spur line from the main railroad was nearly two miles long.

Once it had been only a nuclear generating plant, one of the first built to feed electricity to St. Louis, using the power of atomic fission instead of burning oil or coal. But later, two young scientists named Link and Hokusai had founded a whole new field of atomics and had come here to try it out.

It had been discovered at the beginning of nuclear science that uranium was not the heaviest possible element; others of greater atomic weight—such as plutonium and neptunium—could be created by forcing more neutrons into the atoms. But these had a tendency to grow increasingly unstable with the added mass. Some of these trans-uranium atoms would disintegrate almost instantly. But the two scientists had discovered that, if the packing of more particles could be continued, eventually a new level could be reached where the elements produced became increasingly stable again. Such atoms—super-heavies—had never existed in nature, but many had characteristics that made them extremely valuable.

National had grown to its present size on the development and production of the heavy isotopes, and power was now only a sideline, though the plant supplied all of Kimberly's power requirements.

Ferrel saw Emma stiffen as they neared the gate, but Dick had remembered and was already braking. She had an almost pathological fear of going inside, based on an unrealistic belief that her second child was stillborn because of radiation here. Her worst nightmares centered around the plant. But Doc had long since given up any attempt to reason with her, and she had learned to accept his continuing employment there.

He got out, self-consciously shaking Dick's hand, and watched them hurriedly drive off again. Then abruptly the solid familiarity of his surroundings snapped the blue funk he'd been in. The plant was a world by itself, busy and densely populated. Nothing could uproot it. He waved at the grinning guard and went inside, soaking up the sight, sound and smell of it.

The graveled walks were crowded with the usual nine-o'clock mass of young huskies just going on shift, and the company cafeteria was jammed to capacity with men seeking a last-minute cup of coffee. But the men made way for him good-humoredly as he moved among them. That pleased Doc, as always, and all the more because they didn't bother to stop their horse-play as they might have done for another company official. He'd been just Doc to them too long for that.

He nodded back at them easily, pushed through, and went down the walk toward the Infirmary, taking his own time; at his age a man could begin to realize that comfort and relaxation were worth cultivating. Besides, he could see no reason for ruining the good food in his stomach by rushing around in a flurry that gave him no time to digest it. He let himself in the side entrance, palming his cigar out of long habit, though he'd had the *No Smoking* signs removed years ago, and passed through the surgery to the door marked:

ROGER T. FERREL
Physician in Charge

As always, the little room was heavy with the odor of stale smoke and littered with scraps of this and that. His assistant was already there, rummaging busily through Ferrel's desk with the brass that was typical of the man; Ferrel had no objection to it, though; Blake's rock-steady hands and unruffled brain were always dependable in a pinch of any sort.

Blake looked up and grinned confidently. "Hi, Doc. Where the deuce do you keep your lighter fluid? Never mind, got it! . . . Thought you were taking the day off."

"Fat chance." Ferrel stuck the cigar back in his mouth and settled into the old leather chair, shaking his head. "Palmer phoned me at the crack of dawn. We've got an emergency again."

"So you're stuck with it. I don't see why any of us has to show up here—nothing serious ever pops up. Look at yesterday. I had three cases of athlete's foot —better send a memo down to the showers to use extra disinfectant—a boy with a running nose, the usual hypochondriacs, and a guy with a sliver in his thumb! They bring everything to us except their babies, and they'd have them here if they could. Nothing that couldn't wait a week or a month." He snapped his fingers. "Hey, I almost forgot. If you're free tonight, Anne and I are celebrating sticking together ten years. She wants you and Emma with us. Let the kid handle the office tonight."

"Sounds like a good idea. But you'd better stop calling Jenkins the kid." Ferrel twitched his lips in a stiff smile, remembering the time when he'd been as dead-serious as the new doctor; after only a week of real practice it was too soon to learn that destiny hadn't really singled him out to save the world. "He had his first real case yesterday. Handled it all by himself, so he's now Doctor Jenkins, if you please."

Blake had his own memories. "Yeah? Wonder when he'll realize that everything he did by himself came from you. What was it, anyway?"

"Same old story—simple radiation burns. No matter how much we tell the men when they first come in, most of them can't see why they should wear three ninety-five-per-cent-efficient shields when the main converter shield cuts off all but one-tenth per cent of the radiation." Mathematically, it was good sense that three added shields would cut the radiation down to a mere eighty-thousandth of full force, but it was hard to convince the men that multiplying poor shields by the one good one could make that difference. "He managed to leave off his two inner shields and pick up a year's burn in six hours. Now he's probably home, sweating it out and hoping we won't get him fired."

It had been at Number One, the first converter around which National Atomics had built its present control of artificial radioactives, back in the days before Wemrath at Caltech found a way to use some of the super-heavy isotopes as ultra-efficient shielding. Number One had the old, immense concrete shield, but converters were expensive and they still kept it for the gentler reactions; if reasonable precautions were taken, there was no serious danger.

Blake chuckled. "You're getting old, Doc; you used to give them something to sweat about! Well, I'd better check up on the staff—someone might be a minute late, and then where'd we be?"

Ferrel followed him out, spotting young Jenkins in his office, intent over some book. The boy nodded a tight-lipped greeting. Doc returned it, being careful not to intrude on whatever he was studying. Jenkins was at least intelligent and willing to work. A week was too little to tell whether he had the stuff to stay on here or not, but he probably would if his nerves didn't get in the way. He seemed to be nothing but sinews with taut skin drawn over them, and his shock of blond hair fell over the deepest-set blue eyes Doc had ever seen. He looked like a garret-starving young poet, and his nerves seemed as fine-drawn, but he had an amazingly good background of practical studies.

For a moment Doc considered going back to his office and catching a nap in the old chair. There was nothing to do that Blake couldn't handle. The Infirmary was already run the way he wanted it, and he saw no need to change any details for inspection. He could catch a few winks before Palmer called him He started to turn back, then hesitated at the sight of Jenkins. At his stage, the boy might not understand sleeping on the job.

"If anyone needs me, I'll be at Palmer's office," he called out. Jenkins nodded, and Doc went through the side door and down the long walk toward the Administration building, overshadowed by the ugly bulk of the power-generating station—the oldest building on the grounds. It was squat and massive, and the concrete had weathered to a uniform dirtiness that showed its age. The newer converters were also housed in concrete shells, but the use of super-heavy metal shielding had permitted smaller, more graceful domes.

Palmer's office had been designed to look like a proper place for an executive, including a built-in bar. But in the middle of it, serving as desk, was an old draftsman's table, littered with graphs, stained with ink and loaded with baskets. One corner showed the years of whittling where Palmer had chipped off improvised toothpicks, before he got his complete plates. The man himself was like his office. Tasteful, expensive clothes, a well-barbered look and the obvious intelligence in the heavy face suggested the good executive. But now his suit coat lay on a leather couch and he was wearing a battered leather jacket. His hands bore the marks of hard labor, which had thickened the veins and swelled the knuckles; and he remained as hard-muscled and active in body as a working construction engineer. He nodded Ferrel to a chair, but continued standing himself.

"Thanks for coming, Doc. I got the word late last night. There's even a National Atomic Control Commission inspector with them, ready to snatch our power license if we aren't good boys. I don't mind him; the NACC plays as straight as anyone in government can. But the rest of them—the Guilden reporters, anyhow—are probably looking for trouble. I need every good man here I can get."

"It doesn't make sense," Doc protested. "They can't get along without the plants now; every hospital in the country would go crazy if we stopped production, and it's just as bad with the other users. They can't move the plants out where no workers would come."

Palmer sighed wearily. "They couldn't pass prohibition, either, Doc. But they did."

"But atomic plants aren't that dangerous!"

"Unfortunately, some of them may well be," Palmer said. He looked dead with fatigue, and his reddened eyes indicated that he'd probably had no sleep at all. "We've had fission power for a long time now. That means some of the early plants, built before we knew what we were doing—I helped construct some of them—are probably in bad condition. It also means that a whole generation of workers, engineers and inspectors have been taking them for granted and getting careless. Some of the plants, built when the old AEC was on a reactor binge, were always a bit marginal. Since that accident at Croton, inspections have shown too much radioactive contamination around half a dozen plants. They all need a lot of policing."

"You sound as if you half agreed with the Guilden editorial," Doc protested doubtfully.

Palmer shrugged. "Doc, if moving the plants would solve anything, I'd be all for it. But it's no answer. Once a reactor pile is set up and put into operation, it's already too hot to move. It will be too hot for thousands of years. And if it's abandoned and given no maintenance, it will simply deteriorate faster, increasing the danger. It's like the problem of getting rid of the radioactive wastes from fission reactors. In all the time since Fermi split the atom, nobody has found a safe answer. Every honest engineer and scientist in the business knows that. Until we get cheaper and more efficient fusion plants—ones that aren't so massive they're unable to compete—we're on the edge of disaster."

Doc frowned. He'd rarely spoken to Palmer about such things, and some of the man's attitudes surprised him. "But we're using fusion equipment in some of the converters. The installations didn't look that massive to me."

"Those aren't," Palmer agreed. "We can afford to use fusion inefficiently. We use the fusing hydrogen to get a bigger supply of neutrons to pump into the converters, not for power."

He dropped onto the couch, shoving piles of government bulletins aside and massaging his temples. "I think we're clean here, Doc. But it's just our tough luck that old man Guilden got a tiny dose of poisoning from one of our early products he was misusing. He's gunning for us, using this as a front, and he swings a lot of weight. Oh, hell, I didn't want you for sympathy. I want to check on a probable ringer."

During the early days the companies had been plagued by suits alleging ruined health from radiation poisoning. A few had been legitimate, but most had been phonies trying to force a settlement with the threat of publicity for the company—ringers.

"Plant worker?" Doc asked. They were the hardest to check, since almost any worker would have some slight trace of contamination.

"Delicatessen worker in Kimberly. I talked to her at her place last night, and I think she believes she's been poisoned. But somebody's using her. Expensive lawyer. He wouldn't give her doctor's name. I got her to give her symptoms—and she looks sick."

He passed over a piece of paper covered with his square, heavy writing. Ferrel studied it, trying to make sense out of what a layman considered the facts. Yet there was something of a pattern there. "I'd need more than that, at least a good blood sample, as a start," he protested.

"I've got it. I had that nurse of yours—Dodd—come with me, posing as my secretary. She bullied the woman into giving a sample while I was outside pretending settlement with the lawyer. Here." He handed over a bottle, and Doc could see that Dodd had been careful to make a good job of it. She would, just as she'd been able to persuade the woman to do something without consulting her lawyer. "I'll expect a report on that, after this inspection mess. But what's your guess now?"

Doc gave it reluctantly. "It might be radiation. We can't police every place that uses our stuff. But it's probably leukemia. If she found some slipshod doctor who'd stopped keeping up with progress as well as with professional ethics, he might decide it could fool a jury. It wouldn't, of course."

"It wouldn't have to. We can't take a thing like this to court now. The publicity would ruin us, even if we were proved innocent later. And we can't settle; that would only make us look as if we were guilty." Palmer got up and started pacing about. "That's the trouble, Doc. One little accident that happens—or that might happen—is enough to prove danger. But there's no way to prove the absence of danger in a spectacular fashion that will hit the press. And I can't even swear that there is no danger! . . . . Leukemia . . . cancer of the blood cells. . . ."

"Well, something like that. It used to be one hundred per cent fatal. It still will be if she has it and doesn't get treatment soon."

Palmer breathed a heavy sigh of relief. *"Whew!* At least there's a chance, then. If that's it, we can get a specialist who'll scare her with the facts. She ought to jump at a chance to ditch her lawyer for free treatment. Thanks, Doc. And let me know as soon as you find out for sure."

Ferrel went back to the Infirmary, frowning. If some unethical quack was trying to use the woman, he wanted the man's name. It took only a few of those to ruin the carefully built reputation of the whole profession! He was almost to the corner of the building before he saw Jenkins. The younger doctor was outside, arguing with Jorgenson, one of the top production engineers. Jorgenson was a huge man, nearly seven feet tall, built like an ox, and almost as strong, from the stories told about him, but his mind wasn't secondary to his body.

Jenkins said something quickly, indicating a piece of paper in his hands, but Jorgenson brushed it aside with a flip of his finger. "And I say to hell with you, sonny, until you can make it stick. Go peddle your nostrums!"

The engineer swung around and stalked off. Jenkins stared after him tensely, then stepped back into the Infirmary.

Doc could make no sense of it, but he didn't like it. If the boy was a troublemaker . . . Still, he had nothing to go on. Until he knew more, it was none of his business.

By the time Ferrel was inside, Jenkins had settled back to his usual stiff calm. He looked up at Doc, and his voice was normal. "I've told the nurses to expect more minor accidents already, Dr. Ferrel," he said. "I knew you'd want that, after seeing Mr. Palmer."

Ferrel studied the young man. "Why? Just what was I supposed to have seen Palmer about, anyhow?"

Jenkins controlled his impatience with the older man's obtuseness by an effort, but his voice was respectful. "The inspection, of course. It's all over the plant grapevine. I heard about it when I first came in.

| 16 |

It isn't hard to know what that will do to the accident rate."

"Yeah." Doc grimaced at his own stupidity. He *had* been obtuse. "Good work, son. You were quite right."

There'd be accidents, all right. With men getting a major inspection under these conditions, they'd be under constant tension, and there was no better breeding ground for mistakes. With luck, there might only be the routine mishaps. But there was no way of being sure of such good fortune. Almost anything could happen.

Palmer had indicated that one accident could prove their lack of safety. They certainly couldn't afford any black marks on the books of the committee now. But with any operation as complicated as the creation of the super-heavy isotopes, something was sure to go wrong when the men were on edge.

He should have told Palmer to go to hell and stayed home!

chapter 2

FERREL FOUND Meyers on duty in the dispensary, handling the routine cases with her usual efficiency. He preferred the grim, hard-faced Dodd in the operating room, but here Meyers was best. She was hardly thirty and would have been pretty, except that her face lacked all color. Hair, skin and eyes were all so dull that no amount of make-up could quite bring them to life.

She was swabbing out the eye of a man as Ferrel came in, and she finished before turning to the doctor. "He brushed a cigarette against his eye while putting on his goggles," she reported. "Nothing serious, though. That's the eleventh report I've filled out in the last half hour."

Doc looked at the stack of cards, and his question was answered. Jenkins had been right; the accident rate was triple what it should have been. But so far none of the cases had been serious.

"Not many goldbricks today, though," she said. There were usually a few who decided the best way to get a day off was to play sick. She giggled faintly. "Dr. Jenkins got a run of them, but I guess they didn't like his giving out laxatives. Even the telephone girl wasn't in here today."

"She only reports in sick when she's bored. Today she's probably expecting fireworks," Ferrel observed. He had made it a habit for years to give the girl a day off about once every four months to encourage her imagination. She was the only one in the plant who managed to come up with interesting symptoms when she wanted a day's loafing.

"Jenkins had her yesterday. He diagnosed it as galloping *lethargica gravis* and gave her something that made her lips turn blue for hours," Meyers said. She seemed to admire the boy. It was the first evidence Doc had that Jenkins possessed a sense of humor.

He went back into the main part of the building. They were equipped and staffed beyond any plant set-up he'd ever known, with almost an embarrassment of riches. Aside from Dodd and Meyers, there were three other nurses, two male attendants, two drivers for the little three-wheeled emergency litters, a receptionist, and a secretary for the doctors. The operating room had everything, and there were even little wards where they could keep patients, if the need should arise.

He went over to the hypothermy-cryotherapy outfit, looking down at it. Most of the things here were required by state law, but this was Palmer's own idea. It was designed to lower the temperature of the body —or any part—to a level where there would be no response to pain. It was an old idea in medicine and had been tried for everything, including the attempt to cure cancer. But it had finally been perfected in form, and a technique had evolved that made it usable. In emergency operations it served far better than the usual anesthesia. There was even an attachment for the litter to start freezing tissue on the way in.

The inspection didn't worry him too much. The state laws had been toughened up for atomic plants until they were far more severe than any requirements the NACC might suggest, and he'd passed that inspection less than a month before.

Blake came by, chuckling, and stopped as he spotted Ferrel. "The inspection committee is here, Doc." He was grinning from ear to ear. "But not the reporters! Old Palmer's a fox. He put Number One to work first thing this morning on something the army ordered. It's secret enough so that he could declare the plant restricted territory—but not too restricted for congressmen. So the newspaper boys are running around trying to get themselves cleared. With luck, they'll make it about the time the whole thing's finished."

Doc grinned, but he had his doubts. The men for the Guilden chain would write up what they wanted to, anyhow, and this would only antagonize the reporters who might have been friendly. It would also go rather badly with a couple of the congressmen who apparently were on the committee only for the publicity they could get. To the larger number of men, who were probably quite sincere, it would have a suspicious tinge of trying to cover up from the public.

Palmer usually had his reasons for what he did, but Doc could make little sense of this. It almost seemed that the manager had gone out of his way to make enemies and lose friends.

But at least it was a good story. Even Dodd was smiling when he saw her. On a sudden hunch Ferrel went outside and walked down to the cafeteria. There was only a small crowd there now, but he could catch bits of their conversation as he waited for his coffee. Most of the talk seemed to be about the fate of the reporters. And the general reaction was that Palmer had pulled his best trick in a long time.

Doc headed back, carrying an extra coffee for Meyers, who should need it. She was the only one who'd really been busy so far. He found her alone. "Business slacking off?" he asked as he gave her the container.

"Thanks, Dr. Ferrel. You're a life-saver!" She poured in enough sugar to make a concentrated syrup and sipped the hot stuff gratefully. "I guess I'm losing my popularity. Nobody's been here for the last twenty minutes."

Ferrel hung around a few minutes more, and then left, convinced that his hunch had been right. Palmer had been as aware as Jenkins that the men had spread the story of the inspection and that it was raising hob with morale. He'd been prepared for it, and had made the only possible move to counteract—give the men something to laugh about instead of fretting. Whether it would work when the actual inspection began was another matter.

Dood brought word of the inspection back. Apparently the group was larger than Doc had thought.

There were half a dozen congressmen and a number of "experts" with them. Outside, others were moving about with instruments, making spot checks to find whether the atmosphere and ground around were contaminated. That part of it, at least, was a sensible precaution, though it merely duplicated the checks that National ran periodically itself.

They had already gone through two of the converters with no trouble and not even a minor accident to mar the record. They showed no sign of heading for the Infirmary yet, though Doc had expected that to be one of the first places they would visit. He glanced at the clock and saw that it was already noon.

He went out to locate Dodd and ask for further details, but she could add little to her previous account. The members of the committee were moving about at random now, apparently examining the shipping department.

He fumed for fifteen minutes more. It was his bitten cigar that finally made him realize his tension. He had mangled the end until it finally came to pieces in his mouth. He spat out the tobacco, muttering to himself.

It wasn't the men who were being inspected who would give trouble, nor those who'd already passed, he realized. It was the group who would have to go on waiting, not knowing when their turn would come. He himself had nothing to fear, and yet it was beginning to get him. . . .

He headed for the front office, wondering whether anyone there had heard anything about the future schedule. The receptionist and secretary would be the logical ones to have buddies working in Administration, and even a hint would be helpful. He came through the door just as a wiry little man entered from outside, taking off his Homburg and fiddling with his tiny mustache as he approached the receptionist. Ferrel recognized him just as he looked up.

"Hi, Ferrel," the little man cried.

"Busoni! What are you doing here?" But Doc could guess the answer to that.

It was what he expected. "Serving as expert. I'm your inspector. I've been looking forward to a crack at you too, ever since I knew you were on the list. How's blood-washing?"

"Beats general practice—or it did until you came in, bone-breaker." Busoni had been in Ferrel's class at medical school, specializing in work on fractures. He'd made something of a reputation from his work in re-breaking and correcting old, badly knit fractures. Then he'd built a second reputation from his work in finding ways to wash the radioactive ions out of the calcium of the bones without hurting the calcium deposits themselves. Doc had sent him a patient once after the usual routine with blood-exchange and treatment with the versene group of chemicals had failed.

He held the door while the other walked in. Busoni moved about, taking in the equipment, studying the layout, and moving toward the nurses' toilet. He made a thorough inspection there, nodded, and began marking his sheets. "You pass, Ferrel. Any man who can keep a ladies' room clean has a good mark in my book."

He smiled as he said it, but Doc wasn't sure but what he meant it. At that, the man had managed to cover the key points. Then he snapped his book shut and relaxed. "I got you off lightly, Roger. I told them I knew you, and they figured you'd spill more dirt to me than anyone else. I know better, but why disillusion them? But I'm afraid this plant is in for pretty rough treatment. The committee's mostly pretty honest, but they've been filled with a lot of dirty rumors about Palmer. How about it—does he stink, or does he deserve a break?"

"I'm still here," Ferrel told him. "In fact, I'm here when I could have had the day off."

Busoni grinned. "I'll take that answer. But I don't think I can sell it to anyone else. He made a bad mistake in getting the reporters kicked out. Oh, I can guess why. But a couple of the men feel spiteful, and——"

From outside came the rising wail of an electric siren, reaching a shrill scream that cut through the walls and pierced the ears. Emergency! And from the warbling that was beginning, it meant an emergency with hot stuff floating free!

"Dr. Ferrel!" the paging speaker shouted. "Phone!"

He snatched up the receiver. "Ferrel!"

"Point Twenty!" Palmer snapped the words out, and then hung up. But it was information enough. "Point Twenty"—the pile that gave them their power—and of all the places for an accident Doc liked that least.

He grabbed his emergency bag from the wall and headed for the rear. Dodd was with him, holding out his surgeon's smock. He shook his head, but she clutched it grimly as she ran. In the back receiving room, Beel already had the little litter equipped with twin stretchers, and the motor turning over. He waited until Ferrel and Dodd had grabbed the handrails; then he gunned away, while the second driver was still waiting for Blake and his nurse. Doc ran his eye over the equipment that had been made ready, and nodded. Jones had proved his worth as a male attendant long before, and he was still doing the right thing instantly.

Then for the first time he became aware of the fact that Busoni was riding the litter with him. "Hot stuff!" Doc shouted warningly over the wail of the litter siren. But he was glad to have another doctor at his side.

Crowds were heading for the converter, heedless of the risk, driven by the compulsion to witness disaster. Their presence would make rescue operations more difficult, but the guards were on duty, chasing them back. A vehicle that looked like a fireman's hook-and-ladder engine gunned past at top speed. Its complicated superstructure was like a gigantic, multi-jointed lobster claw, and a man in heavy shielding rode at each end to steer it.

The emergency truck stopped at the side entrance of the huge building that housed the pile. At one time this pile had been the largest commercial fission reactor in existence, and it still ranked high. It broke U-235 down, using part of the broken cores of atoms to turn the more common U-238 into plutonium, from which the pile derived most of its power. Unlike some of the early plants, the pile was not only a power source, but a breeder pile as well, and that made it useful for the production of small amounts of other normal radioactive elements, such as the radioactive potassium that was being separated out at the time of the accident.

The heat generated in the process was piped out, first by liquid sodium, then by exchange to steam, and finally into the huge turbines that generated all the thousands of kilowatts needed to keep the plant going, maintain Kimberly, and even serve as an auxiliary power source for other sections.

But now the red flag was up, which meant that all the damper rods would be in, cutting its power, and letting the men escape through the entrances.

There was one entrance, however, that seemed to have given trouble. The complicated grapple was being backed in as the litter came to a stop. It had to go in, carrying massive shielding for the men—who were also wearing shielded suits—and then to adapt to the angles of the passage. As in all the piles, the escape halls were built with a number of right-angle turns, on the theory that loose radiation travels in straight lines, and that little of it would bounce—while a man could move in zigzag fashion, reaching safer and safer territory.

Abruptly, the grapple began moving out, as rapidly as the men riding the sections could guide it through the passage. Other guards in shields were clearing the area, and now one came up to Doc, holding out a huge, heavy suit. Doc grimaced, but began working his way into it. "What happened?"

"I only got part of it," the guard reported. "Seems they were pulling a thimble of hot stuff out for the Kimberly hospital. One of the men dropped the tongs. The stuff ran all over the floor, or something. One guy didn't get out."

Doc saw that Dodd, Busoni and Blake were in suits by now, and snapped his helmet shut. The grapple came free, holding a limp figure at the end of padded tongs. It swung around, putting the figure into a shielded and padded box.

Busoni was beside Doc as he moved forward. Beel, now also in a suit, was backing the litter, and equipment was being pulled off before Doc could reach the casualty.

"How long?" he asked.

Mervin, the pile superintendent, had been checking, and now answered, his voice muffled through the diaphragm on his helmet. "Six minutes. The alarm wasn't tripped at once, for some reason. Best I can find out is that he saw the thimble falling and caught it in his gloves. He threw it into the hot-pot, clamped the lid down, and then headed for the port that had been left open from the pile. He must have got at least half a minute's dose."

Doc felt sick. Half a minute! It might have been better for him to have died in the chamber.

They were working together now, Dodd, Busoni and Blake with him, fitting the unconscious body with all the things to begin exchanging his blood, pumping out the old and replacing it completely with freshened blood, according to the tattooed type on his wrist. Dodd had him stripped, and the shielded box was being fitted with sprays to wash him free of outside contamination, if any.

Then Doc stopped, gazing at him more closely. The man was Clem Mervin, the super's son! The face of the elder Mervin was almost invisible behind his helmet, but now he nodded slowly at Doc's sudden questioning glance. He'd known all along.

"We'll save him," Doc promised. It was almost certainly true—as far as his life was concerned. Men could be saved from tremendous doses now. But just staying alive was not everything; the boy would go through a year of hell, as a bare beginning, and would certainly be sterile. And his mind was likely to be irreparably harmed.

There was no use lying about that to Mervin; the super knew that himself.

A tiny tanklike car had gone into the passage, dragging hoses to wash out the chamber. Now it came out, and the red flag on the pile building began going down. Apparently the radiation was down to safe levels in the pile chamber, thanks to the sacrifice Clem Mervin had made. Getting the thimble of precious but deadly stuff into the disposal hamper and shutting the port that was open into the pile had kept the level from going too high.

Mervin seemed to gather himself together. "Doc, do what you can, anyway! I've got to get back and salvage that potassium before somebody at Kimberly hospital dies for lack of it."

He moved off, collecting his crew. Doc signaled the waiting ambulance and men began to lift the heavy casketlike box containing the unconscious man while Ferrel and the others shucked off their armor. This was a case for the Kimberly hospital radiation ward. It was smaller than the Infirmary, but they were better equipped for the long, slow process of keeping the man alive.

Doc started to climb into the truck, but Blake stopped him. "Go on back, Doc. I'll take this hitch."

It was just as well. Doc stepped back, watching the vehicle roll off with a scream from its siren. He'd have to drop by the hospital from time to time, but there was nothing more he could do at the moment. Tissue that badly damaged could be repaired only by months of treatment.

Busoni walked beside him silently as they headed back to the litter. But a group of half a dozen men stood in their way. One of them stepped forward.

"Is this the way you usually handle cases, Doctor?" he asked savagely. "Give them a lick and promise and then turn them over to someone else?"

The other men gasped, and moved toward the man. But Busoni was there first. "Shut up, damn you!" he said harshly, and his little figure was shoving the heavy-jowled man aside, pushing him back and out of Ferrel's way. He climbed into the litter with Doc, leaving the congressional committee staring after him. The others turned to the man who had spoken, but Doc had no interest in what they might say or do.

"He'll ache for my scalp for a while, but Morgan will calm him down, Roger," Busoni said. He was grinning wryly now. "Tomorrow we'll both have to apologize and shake hands. And the funny thing is, with them that probably will end it. I won't get into trouble, so forget it. Just be thankful that most of our representatives aren't like him. The committee will go along with me when I say you did a damned fine job. And they'll probably make sure that your Mervin gets a medal."

Doc nodded wearily; it didn't matter too much. He hadn't been worried about any report that might be issued on his work in the affair. Technically it had been a routine accident, and the handling had been efficient and normal. He knew that, and he knew his staff would take it for granted. They simply hadn't been able to work the miracle needed to give immediate assurance of life and health to a boy who'd proved his right to them. No present amount of medical knowledge could do that. But until such miracles could be made to order, the rewards of his job would always be too small for him.

Then he shrugged it off, burying it with the other bitter cases that lay stored in the back of his mind. Someday they might pile up beyond what he could stand, and then he'd be old. But so far he could carry them. He shook Busoni's hand when the litter came to a stop, making the usual meaningless remarks about getting together at the next medical convention. But they probably never would. The difference between a general practitioner and a famous research physician was too great.

He watched carefully to see that the equipment that had come too near young Mervin was put into the decontamination chamber. And finally he turned toward the administration building to report to Palmer. The manager would already have received the general report, but he'd want to know more of what chance the injured man might have and what could be done for him.

And maybe he'd need someone he knew near him as he realized that the one accident that could spell the end of all chances to establish the plant's safety had already occurred. It might be routine here but, to the men who had never seen any atomic accident before, it could be nothing but the final proof that everything related to atomics was dangerous and that the plants weren't safe near civilization.

Doc wondered how Emma would take the move —if the plant *could* be moved.

chapter 3

ALLAN PALMER had learned long before that the place for a manager was in his office.

It had been a long and expensive lesson, but he'd finally accepted the fact. From his desk he could do the one job that nobody else could do and which could only be done from there—he could manage! If he went out to perform deeds of derring-do, the men might love him for it, but they would also suffer, because who would get the work done?

It was one of the secrets that had carried him up the ladder from construction engineer working under a seventh sub-assistant to head of his own atomic-pile construction company—and then to taking over when bad management had almost wrecked National. It was from his desk that he'd persuaded Link and Hokusai to try their new ideas on super-heavy isotopes in full scale, and swung the incredible sums needed to build them the first converter. It was from here that he hoped someday to see Hokusai create a fuel that would take men to the outer planets and back.

Now he listened to Ferrel's account silently, fighting back the old desire to go charging out in a last-ditch effort to prove somehow the safety of the plant before the committee could leave. He saw the strain on Doc's face, and long experience with the man had taught him enough to guess most of the reason—Ferrel's concern for him; Doc hadn't yet realized what personal stakes were involved for himself and all the rest.

Palmer leaned back, looking out of the window toward Kimberly. If the crackpots won, it would be a ghost town in five years; there was no reason for a city of the present size there, without cheap power and without the atomic plant upon which local industry depended. What would Doc get for his house then? How could he send his boy on through college on what a general practitioner could earn in a dying city? And what would happen to Doc's partially crippled wife in whatever wild location would be left within the restrictions of the law they proposed for the plants?

Even Doc wouldn't escape the tar-brush. Let the crackpots win, and every man who was associated with atomics would be a pariah. Doc wasn't too old yet to go back to hospital work, but he couldn't carry the stigma that would go with him. And there were a thousand men or more like Doc out there. They called it *his* problem, but he was the only one among them who was safe, if he chose to give up and sell out for whatever pittance the equipment here might bring. His own private money was secure. He could go to Europe, retire . . .

And let the damned fools who talked about moving atomic plants try to move a pile that had been running for twenty-five years, building up radioactivity within it every second of that time! Let the untended pile erode until the hell inside it broke out, and the people really had contamination on their hands!

"Doc," he said at last, "you've been with me at least twenty years. During that time have I ever lied to you?"

He didn't need the touch of a smile to know the answer to that. The need for absolute truth, no matter how much it hurt, was another of the lessons Palmer had learned long ago. Now he leaned back, forcing his face to a relaxation he couldn't feel. "Okay, then. For God's sake stop deciding I'm all washed up. When I'm licked I'll tell you so! Maybe I'm in a corner now because of the accident, and maybe I couldn't afford it. But I knew it was coming—in these conditions, it had to come; all we could hope was that nobody got hurt, or at least not too many. Maybe it's going to cost more than we can afford, but not more than I'll find a way to pay. They haven't moved us yet, and while I'm alive they won't! That's a promise. Now go home and get some rest, or at least get some rest here and stop thinking about my troubles."

He watched Doc go down the walk toward the Infirmary and nodded slowly to himself. If he'd told the first lie in more than twenty years, he'd done it in a good cause. Doc seemed a dozen years younger than the tired, beaten man who'd come up that walk. And maybe it wasn't a lie. Maybe he could still scrape by, somehow. If not . . .

He stood up and went over to the wall, studying the chart that listed the customers of National together with quantities.

At the top of the list were the hospitals, not because they bought in quantity but because their needs would always have priority. Below that came the military branches, the utilities, the rocket experimenters who needed super-heavy isotopes to line their jets, because nothing else could stand the temperatures of the latest fuels—and below them every major endeavor of the world. In twenty-five years, super-heavy isotopes had become an integral part of the whole fabric of civilization. And now they wanted to rip it out—as if any major industry could move away from all cities of more than ten thousand population. Within six months after the relocation there'd be a city three times that size nearby; there had to be, to hold the workers and the butchers and bakers and shoemakers the workers had to have! And that didn't count the other industries needed to keep National itself running!

His secretary's soft voice spoke from the intercom. "Representative Morgan is here to see you, Mr. Palmer."

"Send him in, Thelma," he told her. Morgan was the best man on the committee, the only one who could see the facts. Idly, though, Palmer was thinking only of the man's white hair again, wondering whether he bleached it to get such a startling effect.

But the rest of the man was almost as impressive. Buried in the files, Palmer had the almost forgotten fact that Morgan had spent several years on the stage under another name as a leading man before turning to law and politics. He was still a consummate actor when he chose, and his speeches were always an event. Now, though, he was acting as little as he could. He looked tired. And the hand he held out lacked some of its usual heartiness.

"I suppose the others have all gone?" Palmer asked.

Morgan nodded. "They pulled out fifteen minutes ago. They got what they came for. Oh, most of them are honest, Allan. Even Shenkler believes the rot he keeps ranting. But that accident's going to make it a lot easier for them to go along with all the voters in their states who are agitating for the bill. It was a tough break."

"Maybe. At least the Guilden papers won't have

pictures of the accident. I'm that much ahead," Palmer told him. "Call it a calculated risk. When you told me last night they were planning this inspection I couldn't guess whether it was better now or later. I still don't know, and it's a little late to change our minds. Bourbon?"

At Morgan's nod, he poured the drinks, mixing his own with a touch of color to make it stronger in appearance than fact.

"What's on your mind, Phil?" he asked.

Morgan laughed. It was a rich, warm laugh that he was accused of having spent years perfecting, but too easy to be anything but his own. It fitted the soft voice and the Southern drawl that could take on a heavy accent when he campaigned in the back counties. "Getting elected again," he admitted easily. "And at the same time keeping a bunch of fools from wrecking us because they're whipped up right now. What happens if the bill doesn't get passed out of committee, Allan? Say for a couple of years?"

It would kill it, Palmer knew. The Croton accident and the discoveries of other contamination had played into the hands of the relatively few real bigots. With two years more to go, the plants would be policed, the people would begin to feel safe again, and the whole movement would die away like most crazes. It was the answer, of course—the quiet, indirect answer that had saved the country repeatedly from some folly, while the papers screamed at the faults of the system that made it possible. And Morgan was head of the committee that would have to submit the bill with recommendations to Congress.

"I'm listening," Palmer said. "But can you get away with it?"

"Not that directly. But I can hold meetings, stall, discuss alternate plans—that sort of thing. The only problem is time." Morgan studied his glass, running the whiskey around in a little swirl that made its beads dance in the sunlight. He shook his head slowly. "Phil, you may not believe it, but I happen to think the country's welfare is more important than I am. If my bottling it up would kill the bill, I'd do it. But to keep it bottled, I have to get re-elected four months from now. That would give us the two years. I'm lucky, in a way. Mississippi's still pretty much an agricultural state, and we don't have much atomic stuff there. So maybe the voters would go along with me if I forgot to report the bill out."

He took another swallow and sighed, either from pleasure or from his own thoughts. "Maybe! But I don't know. Unless I can go back to them and show them I'm doing something for them that means more than any old bill like this. That's where you come in."

"How?"

"Mind you, I'm not guaranteeing I can swing it. If things really get hot enough, they can force the bill onto the floor, no matter what I try! All I can promise is to try to keep it from a vote."

"I know all that," Palmer agreed. He'd been making the reservations as a matter of course.

"Got a copy of that little old house organ of yours?"

Palmer found one on his desk and handed it across, wondering if Morgan realized the little old house organ was the leading scientific paper in the field. Then he blinked as he saw the article the politician was pointing to. Either Morgan knew a lot more about mathematics and engineering than he'd suspected or the man had someone on his side who did.

"Takes a long time to clear the land of the latest mutated form of the weevil down home," Morgan said. "This claims a way to do it in four months. And in four months, if I show the farmers the land free and ready to use again, they'll vote me in even if they see me spit on Lee's picture or find out I've turned atheist. I can get the money for it—don't worry about that. And I can't get 'em to give me 100,000 acres for the experiment. All I need is enough of this to treat that much territory and I'll kill the bill."

The manager studied the map Morgan gave him, estimating the amount. Enough to make a full converter load—two converters to be sure. "But it isn't in production yet," he protested. "Jorgenson ran a test, and he's worked out the engineering techniques for the converters. We can't guarantee conversion efficiency, or——"

"Get me even a quarter of it to start, with the rest coming, and I'll still make out."

Palmer studied it again. He wanted to talk about it to Hokusai and consult with some of the other men. But there'd be no time. If it was to do any good in Morgan's election it would have to start feeding into supply dumps almost at once. "Let me call in Jorgenson and talk it over," he suggested. "If we can do it at all, I'll start changing the converters at once and we'll run an extra shift tonight. Okay?"

"Your word's all I want." Morgan stood up, finished the last of the whiskey and held out his hand. "And now I'd better get back to my colleagues before they smell something."

Palmer watched him go and stood staring at the paper. He shrugged finally and ordered Thelma to locate Jorgenson for him. The mathematics here was beyond his knowledge of modern converter technology; he would have to depend on his production engineer. There was no time for the study others would need in order to form an opinion.

For the hundredth time he cursed the fact that Kellar was dead. The man had been his chief competitor, and had threatened to become more than that. But he'd been a genius, the only man who ever combined engineering talent with the ability to think in the pure mathematics of the abstract scientist and do both by an almost instinctive reaction. He'd have given a lot to be able to call Kellar up and get a snap judgment. But Kellar was dead and the only man who'd ever worked under him was Jorgenson.

Jorgenson was there almost at once, seeming to fill the room. He listened as Palmer outlined the situation. "It'll be a tough job," he said in his slow voice. "This requires a pretty radical change in the converter set-ups, and I'd have to spend a couple of hours briefing my foremen. What converters?"

"You pick them. They're all clean except Number One and Number Six."

"Three and Four, then. It'll be tough enough running two at once on a new project, but I guess I can do it. It's going to cost for some of the materials I'll need, though."

Palmer grinned wryly. It always cost, and if the engineers had a free hand the costs would make profit impossible for the next ten years on any process. But for once the price didn't matter. Jorgenson couldn't spend even a fraction of what success in this would be worth. "Forget the cost, Jorgenson. Do whatever you have to and we'll flange up some kind of accounting later." Then he paused. "If you want to run it."

The huge engineer scowled at him. "Of course I want to run it. Why not?"

"Because you'll be working with a bunch of men who've just seen one accident already today. They'll be tired from that, from the shift they've already put in and from wondering what will happen to them when the committee report goes in. Those men aren't normal workers now, and don't forget it. I can give you twice the number you'll need, to ease the work, but I can't give you fresh, unworried men. Do you still want it?"

"I'll run it."

Then Jorgenson paused, hesitating over a decision. Finally his enormous shoulders hunched. "Look, Palmer, I've been over that math a hundred times and I've run six trial lots in the tank. There isn't a thing I can find wrong anywhere. But since this came out, I'd better mention that there's one vote against the process. Only one—nobody else has been worried. But I figure you should know."

"I should," Palmer agreed. "Who was it?"

"Just an amateur—makes a hobby of atomics, I guess. But he claimed we might get Isotope R."

Palmer felt the skin along his back quiver. The possible existence of Isotope R was enough to make every man in the country get behind the bill, perhaps including Morgan. Sometimes he'd had nightmares of word of it reaching the Guilden press, but so far those who knew about it were the last ones who would leak it to such a place.

"An amateur, and he knows about that?" he asked sharply.

"His old man was in the business," Jorgenson answered. He scowled again, then shrugged once more. "Look, I've been over these figures again since he brought it up. If I thought there was a chance in a billion of R getting mixed up in it you couldn't hire me to touch it. It's not the first time that has come up."

In that the man was right. Palmer had missed his chance at a highly desirable process once simply because a professor had written in suggesting a possible chain that might lead to the dreaded isotope. The small plants that competed weakly with him had run it off with no difficulty and now used it as the backbone of their businesses.

He stared at the chart that showed his outlets again, and then out at the plant. If it meant only the loss of revenue he'd still call a halt until he could have every figure rechecked fifty times more. But this time he was gambling a vague, probably ridiculous fear on the part of someone who was an amateur against the fate of all the plants, and perhaps of any orderly civilization for the next decade.

"All right," he said at last. "Run it."

But he was reaching for the phone before Jorgenson was through the door. "Give me Ferrel," he told the operator.

He had no business asking the man to stay on for the late shift, of course. But he made no move to cancel the call. There was no logic in his decision but he'd learned to follow his hunches when they were this strong.

At least the men would feel better, knowing that Doc was there. They had learned to trust themselves to him. And right now they needed all the comfort they could get.

chapter 4

THE WHISTLE indicating the end of a shift had sounded as Ferrel finished his hasty supper and headed back toward his office. The cafeteria was filled with the usual five-o'clock rush, but now there was a further bustle as those who would be on the graveyard shift headed for it. It wasn't hard now to spot the family men; they were busy with discussions of the amount of overtime they'd draw, while the bachelors were the ones grumbling and swearing at broken dates and ruined plans. If there was any tension left from the day it didn't show, but that was no proof it wasn't there.

He let himself in through the side door. Blake was sitting on a corner of his desk checking through the few memos of the day.

Blake shook his head solemnly, making clucking noises with his tongue. "You're getting old, Doc. Taking a coffee break at this time. And you've forgotten that memo for disinfection of the showers. They're going to need new blood at the top here if this keeps up." Then he stood up, grinning. "Come on, we've still got that celebration to take care of."

"I'm sorry, Blake. Not a chance now." He'd forgotten their tenth anniversary completely, but it was too late to back out on his agreement with Palmer now. "The plant's on overtime, and I've been elected to the graveyard shift. Some rush order for Three and Four."

Blake frowned. "Why can't Jenkins swing it alone? Anne's been counting on you and Emma."

"This happens to be my job. As a matter of fact, though, Jenkins will be staying on with me."

Blake sighed and gave up. "Anne's gonna be disappointed, but she ought to know how it goes. If you get off early, you and Emma drop out and say hello, even if it's after midnight. Well, take it easy."

" 'Night." Ferrel watched him leave and smiled affectionately. Someday Dick would be out of medical school, and Blake would make a good man for him to start under and begin the same old grind upward. First, like young Jenkins, Dick would be filled with his mission to humanity, tense and uncertain, but somehow things would roll along through Blake's stage and up, probably to Doc's own level, where the same old problems were solved in the same old way and life settled down into a comfortable routine with only an occasional bad day, like this one.

There were worse lives, certainly, even though it wasn't like the mass of murders, kidnapings and applied miracles in the movie he'd seen recently on television, where chrome-plated converters covered with pretty neon tubes were mysteriously blowing up every second day and men were brought in with blue flames all over them, cured instantly—to dash out and quench the flame barehanded.

For a moment he wondered whether such films helped create the average man's fear of atomics or simply mirrored it. Probably a little of both, he decided as he dropped into his chair.

Then he heard Jenkins out in the surgery, puttering around with quick, nervous little sounds. Never do to let the boy find him loafing back here when the possible fate of the world so obviously hung on his alertness. Young doctors had to be disillusioned slowly or they became bitter and their work suffered. Yet in spite of his amusement at Jenkins' nervousness, he couldn't help envying the thin-faced young man's erect shoulders and flat stomach. Blake might be right; maybe he was growing old.

Jenkins straightened a wrinkle on his white jacket fussily and looked up. "I've been getting the surgery ready for instant use, Dr. Ferrel. Do you think it's safe to keep only Miss Dodd and one male attendant here? Shouldn't we have more than the legally required minimum staff?"

"Dodd's a one-woman staff," Ferrel said. "Expecting more accidents tonight?"

"No, sir, not exactly. But do you know what they're running off?"

"No." Ferrel hadn't asked Palmer; he'd learned long ago that he couldn't keep up with the atomic engineering developments, and had stopped trying. "Something new for the army?"

"Worse than that, sir. They're making their first

commercial run of Natomic Isotope 713 in both Number Three and Four converters at once."

"So? Seems to me I did hear something about that. Had to do with killing off the boll weevils, didn't it?" Ferrel was vaguely familiar with the process of sowing radioactive dust in a circle outside the weevil area to isolate the pest, then gradually moving inward from the border. Used with proper precautions it had slowly killed off the weevil and driven it back into half the territory once occupied.

Jenkins managed to look disappointed, surprised and slightly superior. "There was an article on it in the *Natomic Weekly Ray* of last issue, Dr. Ferrel. You probably know that the trouble with Natomic Isotope 544, which they've been using, was its half-life of over a month. It made the land sowed useless for planting the next year, so they had to move slowly. Isotope 713 has a half-life of less than a week and reaches safe limits in about four months, so they'll be able to isolate whole strips of hundreds of miles during the winter and still have the land usable by spring. Field tests with pilot runs have been highly successful and we've just got a huge order from a state that wants immediate delivery."

"After the legislature waited six months debating whether to use it or not," Ferrel hazarded out of long experience. "Ummm, sounds good if they can sow enough earthworms and other soil life afterwards to keep the ground in good condition. But what's the worry?"

Jenkins shook his head indignantly. "I'm not worried. I simply think we should take every possible precaution and be ready for any accident; after all, they're working on something new, and a half-life of a week is rather strong, don't you think? Besides, I looked over some of the reaction charts in the article and——What was that?"

From somewhere to the left of the Infirmary, a muffled growl was being accompanied by ground tremors; then it gave way to a steady hissing, barely audible through the insulated walls of the building. Ferrel listened a moment and shrugged.

"Nothing to worry about, Jenkins; you'll hear it a dozen times a year. Ever since I joined the staff here, Hokusai's been bugs about getting an atomic fuel that can be used in rockets. He isn't satisfied with the progress they've made on the space station—wants to see real payloads carried up. Someday you'll probably see the little guy brought in here minus his head but so far he hasn't found anything with the right kick that he can control. What about the reaction charts on I-713?"

"Nothing definite, I guess." Jenkins turned reluctantly away from the sound, still frowning. "I know it worked in small lots but there's something about one of the intermediate steps I distrust, sir. I thought I recognized . . . I tried to speak to Jorgenson and you can guess what happened. He wouldn't discuss it."

Seeing the boy's face whiten over tensed jaw muscles, Ferrel held back his smile and nodded slowly. If that was what had led to Jorgenson's outburst it was understandable enough. But the whole picture didn't make sense. Jenkins' pride would have been wounded, but hardly as much as seemed to be the case. There was something funny behind it and someday Ferrel would have to find what it was; little things like that could ruin a man's steadiness with the instruments if he kept them to himself. Meantime the subject was best dropped.

The telephone girl's heavily syllabalized voice cut into his thoughts from the paging speaker. "Dr. Ferrel! Dr. Ferrel wanted on the telephone. Dr. Ferrel, please!"

Jenkins' face went completely white. His eyes

darted to his superior. Doc grunted. "Probably Palmer's bored and wants to tell me how he made out with the union. Or about his grandson. He thinks the child's a genius because he knows a couple of words now."

But inside the office he stopped to wipe his hands free of perspiration before answering. There was something contagious about Jenkins' suppressed fears. And Palmer's face on the phone's little viewer was all wrong. He was wearing a set smile like a mask. Ferrel suspected there was someone else in the office out of sight of the pickup.

"Hi, Ferrel." Palmer's voice also had a false heartiness to it, and the use of the last name was a clear sign of some trouble. "There has been a little accident on one converter, they tell me. They're bringing a few men over to the Infirmary for treatment— probably not right away, though. Has Blake gone yet?"

"He's been gone half an hour or more. Think it's serious enough to call him back, or are Jenkins and myself enough?"

"Jenkins? Oh, the new doctor." Palmer hesitated, and his arms showed quite clearly the doodling operations of his hands, out of sight of the pickup. "No, of course there's no need to call Blake back, I suppose— not yet, anyway. It would only worry anyone who saw him returning. You can probably handle everything."

"What is it—radiation burns or straight accident?"

"Mostly radiation, I think—maybe some accident stuff, too. Someone got careless again. You know what that means; you've seen what happens when one of the high-pressure lines breaks."

Doc had been through that, if that was what it was. "Sure, we can handle that, Palmer. But I thought you had already finished the job you were doing in Number One an hour ago. And how come they haven't installed the pressure reliefs? I thought all that was done six months ago."

"I didn't say it was Number One or that a line broke. I was just comparing it to something familiar. We have to use new equipment for the new products." Palmer looked up at someone else, confirming Doc's idea, and his upper arms made a slight movement before he looked down at the pickup again. "I can't go into it now, Doc; the accident's throwing us off schedule already—details piling up on me. We can talk it over later, and you probably have to make arrangements now. Call me if you want anything."

The screen darkened and the phone clicked off abruptly, just as a muffled word started. The voice hadn't been Palmer's. Ferrel pulled his stomach in, wiped the sweat off his hands again and went out into the surgery with careful casualness. Damn Palmer, why couldn't the fool give enough information to make decent preparations possible? He was sure Three and Four alone were operating, and they were supposed to be fool-proof. Just what had happened?

As he came out, Jenkins jerked up from a bench, face muscles tense and eyes filled with a sure fear. Where he had been sitting a copy of the *Weekly Ray* was lying open at a chart of symbols which meant nothing to Ferrel, except for the penciled line under one of the reactions. The boy picked it up and stuck it back on a table.

"Routine accident," Ferrel reported as naturally as he could, cursing himself for having to force his voice. Thank the Lord, the boy's hands hadn't trembled visibly when he was moving the paper; he'd still be useful if surgery was necessary. Palmer had said nothing about that, of course; he'd said nothing about entirely too much. "They're bringing a few men over for radiation burns, according to Palmer. Everything ready?"

Jenkins nodded tightly. "Quite ready, sir—as much as we can be for routine accidents at Three and

Four! Isotope R . . . Sorry, Dr. Ferrel, I didn't mean that. Should we call in Dr. Blake and the other nurses and attendants?"

"Eh? Oh, probably we can't reach Blake, and Palmer doesn't think we need him. You might have Nurse Dodd locate Meyers—the others are out on dates by now, if I know them, and those two should be enough with Jones; they're better than a flock of the other nurses, anyway." Isotope R? Ferrel remembered the name, but nothing else. Something an engineer had said once—but he couldn't recall in what connection—or had Hokusai mentioned it? He watched Jenkins leave, and turned back on an impulse to his office, where he could phone in reasonable privacy.

"Get me Matsuura Hokusai." He stood drumming on the table impatiently until the screen finally lighted and the little Japanese looked out of it. "Hoke, do you know what they were turning out over at Three and Four?"

The scientist nodded slowly, his wrinkled face as expressionless as his high-pitched English. "Yess, they are make I-713 for the weevil. Why you ask?"

"Nothing; just curious. I heard rumors about an Isotope R and wondered if there was any connection. Seems they had a little accident over there, and I want to be ready for whatever comes of it."

For a fraction of a second the heavy lids on Hokusai's eyes seemed to lift, but his voice remained neutral, only slightly faster. "No connection, Dr. Ferrel; they are not make Issotope R, very much assure you. Best you forget Issotope R. Very sorry, Dr. Ferrel, I must now see accident. Thank you for call. Goodby." The screen was blank again, along with Ferrel's mind.

Jenkins was standing at the door, but had either heard nothing or seemed not to know about it. "Nurse

Meyers is coming back," he said. "Shall I get ready for curare injections?"

"Uh—might be a good idea." Ferrel had no intention of being surprised again, no matter what the implication of the words. Curare, one of the great poisons, known to South American primitives for centuries before it was synthesized by modern chemistry for treatment of certain spastic conditions, was the final resort for use in cases of radiation injury that were utterly beyond control. While the Infirmary stocked it for such emergencies, in the long years of Doc's practice it had been used only twice; neither experience had been pleasant. Jenkins was either thoroughly frightened or overly zealous—unless he knew something he had no business knowing.

"Seems to take them long enough to get the men here; can't be too serious, Jenkins, or they'd move faster."

"Maybe." Jenkins went on with his preparations, dissolving dried plasma in distilled, de-aërated water. He added the ingredients for checking plutonic anemia and liver degeneration without looking up. "There's the litter siren now. You'd better get washed up while I take care of the patients."

Doc listened to the sound that came in as a faint drone from outside, and grinned slightly. "Must be Beel driving; he's the only man fool enough to run the siren when the runways are empty. Anyhow, if you'll listen, it's the out trip he's making. Be at least five minutes before he gets back." But he turned into the washroom, kicked on the hot water and began scrubbing vigorously with the strong soap.

Damn Jenkins! Here he was preparing for surgery before he had any reason to suspect the need, and the boy was running things to suit himself, pretty much as if armed with superior knowledge. Well maybe he was. Either that or he was simply half-crazy with old wives' fears of anything relating to atomic reactions, and that didn't seem to fit the case. As Jenkins came in, Doc rinsed off, kicked on the hot-air blast, and let his arms dry, then bumped against a rod that brought out rubber gloves on little holders. "Jenkins, what's all this Isotope R business, anyway? I've heard about it somewhere, probably from Hokusai. But I can't remember anything definite."

"Naturally—there isn't anything definite. That's the trouble." The young doctor tackled the area under his fingernails before looking up; then he saw that Ferrel was slipping into his surgeon's whites, which had come out on a hanger, and waited until the other was finished. "R's one of the big 'maybe' problems of atomics. Purely theoretical, and none's been made yet —it's either impossible or can't be done in small control batches safe for testing. That's the trouble, as I said; nobody knows anything about it, except that— if it can exist—it'll break down in a fairly short time into Mahler's Isotope. You've heard of that?"

Doc had—twice. The first had been when Mahler and half his laboratory had disappeared with accompanying noise; he'd been making a comparatively small amount of the new product designed to act as a starter for other reactions. His helper, Maicewicz, had tackled it on a smaller scale and that time only two rooms and three men had gone up in dust particles. Five or six years later, atomic theory had been extended to the point where any student could find why the apparently safe product decided to become pure helium and energy in approximately one-billionth of a second.

"How long a time?"

"Half a dozen theories, no real ideas. Look, there are two areas our mathematics can't handle well. One is at the point on the scale where the atoms stop getting progressively more unstable and begin to find new stability in the super-heavy isotopes. That's where Mahler's Isotope exists. And by good luck, in building up in the converters, this is a skip zone—an atom seems to build up to a certain level step-by-step; then it grabs a bunch of neutrons all at once and goes super-heavy. Nobody is sure why. Isotope R and I-713 are at the other end of the scale where we begin to approach the maximum atomic weight we can reach. Up there, the nuclei of the atoms are so complicated that they can do all sorts of things impossible to normal atoms. Apparently, at least from some theories, they can split apart to produce Mahler's Isotope. At least Mahler's experiments were heading along those lines."

Jenkins shrugged, ending the lecture. They had come out of the washroom, finished except for their masks. Jenkins ran his elbow into a switch that turned on the ultraviolets that were supposed to sterilize the surgery, then looked around questioningly. "What about the supersonics?"

Ferrel kicked them on, shuddering as a bone-shaking subharmonic hum indicated their activity. Technicians had supposedly debugged the supersonics twice, but the hum was still there. He couldn't complain about the amount of equipment, though. Ever since the last major accident, when the state congress developed ideas, there'd been enough gadgets around to stock up several small hospitals. The supersonics were intended to penetrate through all solids in the room, sterilizing where the UV light couldn't reach. A whistling note from their generator reminded him of something that had been tickling around in the back of his mind for some minutes.

"There was no emergency whistle, Jenkins. Hardly seems to me they'd neglect that if it was so important."

Jenkins grunted skeptically and eloquently. "With

everyone trying to get Congress to chase all the atom plants out into the middle of the Mojave desert, Palmer would be a fool to advertise the fact that there was another accident."

"There's the siren again."

Jones, the male attendant, had heard it, and was already running out the fresh stretcher for the litter into the back receiving room. Half a minute later, Beel came trundling in the detachable part of the litter. "Two," he announced. "More coming up as soon as they can get to 'em, Doc."

There was blood spilled over the canvas, and a closer inspection indicated its source in a severed jugular vein, now held in place by a small safety pin that had fastened the two sides of the cut with a series of little pricks around which the blood had clotted enough to stop further loss.

Doc kicked off the supersonics with relief and indicated the man's throat. "Why wasn't I called out instead of having him brought here?"

"Hell, Doc, Palmer said bring 'em in, and I brought 'em—I dunno. Guess some guy pinned up this fellow, so they figured he could wait. Anything wrong?"

Ferrel grimaced. "With a torn jugular, nothing that stops the bleeding's wrong, orthodox or not. How many more, and what's wrong out there?"

"Lord knows, Doc. I only drive 'em. I don't ask questions. So long!" He pushed the new stretcher up on the carriage and went wheeling it out to the small two-wheeled tractor that completed the litter. Ferrel dropped his curiosity back to its proper place and turned to the first case, while Dodd adjusted her mask. Jones had their clothes off, swabbed them down hastily, and wheeled them out on operating tables into the center of the surgery.

"Plasma!" A quick examination had shown Doc

nothing else wrong with the man on the table, and he made the injection quickly. Apparently the man was only unconscious from shock induced by loss of blood, and the breathing and heart action resumed a more normal course as the liquid filled out the depleted blood vessels. He treated the wound with an antibiotic in routine procedure, cleaned and sterilized the edges gently, applied clamps carefully, removed the pin, and began stitching with the complicated little motor needle—one of the few gadgets for which he had any real appreciation. A few more drops of blood had spilled, but not seriously, and the wound was now permanently sealed. "Save the pin, Dodd. Goes in the collection. That's all for this. How's the other, Jenkins?"

Jenkins pointed to the back of the man's neck, indicating a tiny bluish object sticking out. "Fragment of steel, clear into the medulla oblongata. No blood loss, but he's been dead since it touched him. Want me to remove it?"

"No need—mortician can do it if he wants . . . If these are samples, I'd guess it as a plain industrial accident, instead of anything connected with radiation."

"You'll get that, too, Doc." It was the first man, apparently conscious and normal except for pallor. "We weren't in the converter house. Hey, I'm all right! I'll be . . ."

Ferrel smiled at the surprise on the fellow's face. "Thought you were dead, eh? Sure, you're all right, if you'll take it easy. Just pipe down and let the nurse put you to sleep, and you'll never know you got it."

"Lord! Stuff came flying out of the air-intake like bullets out of a machine gun. Just a scratch, I thought; then Jake was bawling like a baby and yelling for a pin. Blood all over the place—then here I am, good as new."

"Uh-huh." Dodd was already wheeling him off toward a ward room, her grim face wrinkled into a half-quizzical expression over the mask. "Doctor said to pipe down, didn't he? Well!"

As soon as Dodd vanished Jenkins sat down, running his hand over his cap; there were little beads of sweat showing where the goggles and mask didn't entirely cover his face. " 'Stuff came flying out of the air-intake like bullets out of a machine gun,' " he repeated softly. "Dr. Ferrel, those two cases were outside the converter—just by-product accidents. Inside . . ."

"Yeah." Ferrel was picturing things himself, and it wasn't pleasant. Outside, matter tossed through the air ducts; inside . . . He left it hanging. "I'm going to call Blake. We'll probably need him."

chapter 5

MAL JORGENSON cursed as he moved about in the crushing weight of the big Tomlin suit. The bulk of its multitude of shields and the complicated nonsense of its built-in air system would have killed a lesser man in minutes, so they had to make him the guinea pig to test it. To make matters worse, it added to his stature, until even the ratholes he'd learned to navigate were too small for him. He cursed again, and swore at the pigmy race that had spawned him, with their puny minds even smaller than the silly things they called bodies.

The inside of the converter was a mess. From

the cylindrical sides to the top of the dome, five storeys above the ground, it was jammed with equipment that had been hastily crammed in and jury-rigged in the haste of initiating the project.

He wedged himself into the upper test pit of Number Three, trying to get his shoulders in far enough to hook on his gauge. There'd been no time to install a proper bank of test instruments; they could wait weeks to try his process—and then they expected him to do it all overnight!

Finally, by resorting to pure mathematics, he found a means to insert himself into a position where he could run off a test. The results agreed with what he'd expected, of course. There might be some satisfaction in all this yet—if Palmer stuck around long enough to eat crow for the doubts that had been on his face. There were a few things Jorgenson had been saving to tell him!

He caught his shoulder edging out, and swore hotly, not bothering to turn down the radio on his suit. Damn it, Palmer had no business insisting that everyone wear suits on this job. They only made the work more complicated, and showed the men that the manager didn't trust him. It was standard operating procedure on an initial run, as the manager said. But this was a special job, done on the worst possible short notice. Some concessions might have been made!

He climbed down, his anger bearing him up. He had reason to be angry in a world where nothing fitted, where travel was an ordeal, and where even the clothes he wore had to be built to order at a price that sapped his income and left him with no hope for his future. And the women. . . .

He almost spat, before he remembered the visor in front of his face.

Briggs was standing with a bunch of the men by the south converter safety chamber. The big hulk of the converter was built inside an even bigger housing, made of thick concrete, and the chambers had been designed along the outer housing wall for use in accidents. They were never meant as meeting halls, yet the fools were all huddled about the chambers, as if they had no faith in him.

"Get those runts of yours out on the job, Briggs," he ordered. "I don't want to see them clumped up here again. Damn it, we're running a new job. If I have to change the setting, or if those gauges start to go up, I want to see men where they can move. You've worked with me before. You know what I want."

"You want a knife in the guts some dark night," Briggs said, his voice quiet and cold. "You run your blasted conversion and I'll run the men. Palmer told me to keep them back when I could."

There was nothing Jorgenson could do about it. If he knocked the fool cold for his insolence, the whole pigmy group would be down on him for picking on a smaller man. He'd had trouble enough before—though never this much. If Palmer would back him up . . . But the manager wouldn't. Even Kellar had been hell to work with and soft-headed about the men.

He checked on the readings of the huge magnets and the laser that controlled the neutron injection. Damn that kid Jenkins! The young doctor had to be wrong in his needless fears. Yet now Jorgenson found himself holding down the injection to the minimum, threatening a loss of efficiency in conversion. He should . . . Then he shrugged, letting things stay as they were. At least the man riding the controls was sticking to his duties. Better not change his orders. Jorgenson took a final look at the converter, then nodded unhappily.

He clumped away, heading through the slow-moving, massive door of the housing wall and toward Number Four. It was overdue for a check, as a result of the delay in handling the instruments where there was no room to turn. A good instrument reader might have helped, but he'd never found one he could trust. He stood fuming while the motors in the second converter slowly pushed the entrance wide enough for him to pass through.

Inside Number Four, Grissom was at least some improvement over Briggs. The foreman had kicked, but now he had his men spaced out where they belonged. They looked scared, but it was good for them. A little adrenalin in their blood streams might put some life into them.

"Get that feeder dressed down," he told Grissom. It had been badly hooked up, in spite of the bonus he'd offered that afternoon, and had come partly loose, so that it thumped with the changes in pressure going on inside the converter. But as long as the designers insisted on putting housings around the converters— to hold in the effects of accidents, they claimed—instead of leaving the machinery outside where it could be reached, sloppy work was to be expected.

He climbed laboriously up to the testing pit and went through the whole operation again, figuring out a way to get his arms far enough in to read his gauge. He stared at it automatically and then his eyes focused on it sharply.

The needle wasn't steady.

It was wobbling from side to side, dancing erratically. Its periodic dip and rise reminded him of something else. With a snap, his mind dug out the memory and examined it.

The time was the same as that of the feeder that was loose.

The pressures inside were varying, but he'd expected that. It still should have no effect on the other readings. And yet the fluctuation was obvious.

He flipped the pages of his notes in his head,

running over them as quickly as if they had been on printed sheets. There was nothing there to predict such behavior. It would apply only to an entirely different reaction.

He balanced the new equations that would fit, adjusting them to the facts. It was pressure work—something that would leave his head splitting for hours. He hated it, and he had never quite learned to make it completely trustworthy. But this time something in the back of his mind was shrieking the truth of the new equations.

Jenkins! The damned impertinent kid had pointed to just such an equation! He'd had the nerve to suggest that there was a second possibility Jorgenson had overlooked. And now even the fates were conspiring with the pigmies to prove that he was right and the man who had invented the whole process was wrong!

He screamed through his helmet, calling the attention of the men below him. There was still time, if they worked it right. It was close, but they could make it.

He threw himself forward, almost overbalancing until he could reach the emergency cut-off for the fusion unit. With his other arm, he waved the foreman toward the emergency station.

Grissom stood staring up, like a cowed rabbit. The men watched his gestures with no sign of understanding.

"Get moving!" Jorgenson yelled at them, forcing his helmet amplifier to the limit, draining the batteries savagely. "Pull the main ballast magnets back—all the way back. And give me more current through the primary inductances! Damn you, move! Do you want this whole thing to blow up in your faces? You're going to be dealing with Isotope R in thirty seconds!"

Grissom moved then—the wrong way.

With a frantic scream from his helmet diaphragm,

he dived for the north converter chamber. For a split second, the others hesitated. Then they dropped what they were doing and joined him in the mad race.

It was too late to save anything after that.

Jorgenson saw the door of the safety chamber swinging shut. He estimated it, and knew that they'd have it closed in plenty of time for safety. He also knew he could make it himself before it closed, even in the pressing weight of the heavy suit. He told his legs to jump for it.

And they responded, but not as he had intended! They carried him away from the inner wall, to land at a sickening, jarring run, heading around the converter toward the other men. He saw some of them staring, probably unable to make out his words before, but scared because they had seen others in motion.

"Get into the chamber!" he yelled. Under maximum drain, the amplifier was already failing as the batteries went dead. "Into the chamber!"

They were like helpless sheep as they realized what he was saying. The spineless fools couldn't even save themselves. They had to wait for a better man to sacrifice himself.

He saw them heading for the chamber, and he knew it was almost too late. The anger in him was boiling now, surging through his veins, sending out adrenalin until he no longer felt the weight of the suit. He caught one of the laggards and literally tossed him the ten feet into the safety chamber. But there was no time to save all of them. They were in the way of his own progress.

And if one of them got part way through the door as it was closing, nobody would have a chance; the door had to seal tightly, and it couldn't do that with a body stuck in it. There was barely enough space now for him to make it. If he jumped, kicking back at the two who were threatening to jam the door, he might be able to get in.

But he didn't jump. He swung his big arms down, scooping one of the wretches into the chamber. There was no chance for the other. And there was no hope for life out here in any ordinary suit, even for minutes. The man was clawing at the big door, now too far shut for anyone to enter, trying to slip his arm inside.

All the hate that had filled him for years coursed through Jorgenson. He brought his fist down, twisting the helmet of the man into a pulped ribbon of metal. The arm continued the motion, and the man's body skidded out of the path of the slow-closing door, leaving it free.

The fools inside were screaming and pointing, but he paid no heed to them. He knew the exact second now, as he had known it nearly all his life—the exact fraction of time that had elapsed. It was all that was left of his rational thought.

Right on schedule, he heard the first crack above him like a blow that seemed to torture his eardrums, even through the heavy armor. But he didn't stop to look. The door was finally closing. He put his shoulder to it, bracing his feet, and lunged. It gave a trifle more, speeding up under the combined force of the motor and his muscles. And at last some of the men had seen a trace of reason and were pulling on it, adding their puny strength to his.

The converter broke apart, spilling its contents outward! He saw it flying by him, spitting through the crack in the door. The impact forced him from his position, knocking him sideways. The glare of it made the ending of the lights unimportant, and then the magma was covering his face plate until he couldn't see. He groped his way along the floor, fighting the pressure, until he could feel the door. He found another purchase and began shoving again, trying to will the thing closed. And finally, the crack vanished. He could do no more. Either the idiots inside would live or they'd die, but it was none of his responsibility now.

He relaxed then, surprised by the roaring and hissing going on. He felt something sting near one of the joints of his armor. The stuff was giving off tiny explosions, apparently with enough force to drive through all his armor!

He fought to his feet, ignoring the agony signals from his nerves and refusing to heed the twitching of his muscles. There was only the rage in him now, driving him on. He knew he was going to die, and no longer cared. But this was his process, and he was its master. It would have no victory over him!

Buffeted and beaten, with hell raging all around him and sometimes almost over him, he fought his way ahead, building a complete picture of the converter chamber and everything in it in his mind. There were the tools that had been dropped and photographed by his eyes. There was the corpse of the man he had killed for no better reason than to save others who didn't deserve to live. And then he had it. There was the big lead box that had been brought in to hold the first testing of the results, until it could be certified.

His head ached savagely as he strained his mind to its utmost limit, driving it to handle more factors at once and build a more completely four-dimensional picture of the surroundings than he had ever tried before. He had to picture every movement of his own body, then extend that to the currents and pulses swirling around him, and retranslate that into the motion of the box. It couldn't have moved far, but in the few seconds of time his personal energy would last, he couldn't go hunting for it.

Then the picture solidified. He could see himself and the box in his mind, and even see the side on which the cover was. He moved toward it, and his fingers groped out and located it.

But at that moment, as during his whole life, the fates tricked him. He had located the box, but the lid was at an angle different from his picture. He cursed and screamed to himself in helpless frustration as he realized that the maximum power of his mind had built an imperfect image.

His fingers were moving along the box like little animals with minds of their own, testing it with thumps that carried back messages to his brain. Now he pulled the lid up, grateful that it was on top and the box would need no turning. With the last bit of energy, he let himself inside, solving the problem of the best position to take automatically as he did so. Then he dropped the lid back, trying to force it to a snug fit. He felt the box move under the still active forces of the new matter outside, but he could no longer care.

His mind blanked out.

He came to in hell, with the air hot and thick in his suit, and the sweat trickling out of him, though his body felt dried to the bones. There was a faint surge to the box in which he lay, as if one end were propped up and the other rocking on something.

But the shock that washed through him didn't come from the realization of where he was or what must happen to him. The twitching of his muscles and the certain death that must face him meant very little.

The overwhelming fact was that he'd been insane for years! He turned that over in his thoughts, grappling with it—and accepting it. He'd been going insane by the time he reached adolescence. He had been wholly so before he graduated from college. He had lived in an impossible world where only absolute perfection counted, and where he refused to accept perfection as possible, even to himself! He had built his hate against the impossible into a constant churning force that whipped every tissue of him during all his life.

He'd been berserk! And yet, somehow it had been a cold, hard fury, capable of dissimulating when necessary. He'd kept the fury inside, away from the men over him, and usually within limits that men below him could at least tolerate. There had never been equals. He had reserved the real savagery of his berserk mind for himself.

And now his fury was burned out, unable to stand the gross overload of the last few seconds out there and the fact of the death he had to face. His mind felt empty, yet clearer than it had ever been. The trick of complete visual recall was still there. He could see every page he had ever read. And the ability to construct a full new picture mentally was sharper than before. He had built his life on those tricks—and they had driven him mad when he had learned that their discovery could only result in rejection or petty schemes for exploitation. Now they were only means to an end—not an end in themselves. They were talents that could help him think, not thoughts themselves.

It hurt to be only a man, rather than an angry, crippled god in chains. But he accepted it.

He turned his thoughts to his own situation again, and a faint feeling of fear touched him. He forced it away, as he was forcing away all the pain and anguish that tried to drum into his head. He was in the box, still above the stuff that must be bubbling out there, protected by the strong walls that were layered with lead. So long as he remained above the stuff, where it could not get into the box, he was somewhat safe. He could live until his air ran out, or the sweat drained his body too dry, or the heat finally overcame him. It wouldn't be long.

He wondered about the men. He hadn't known

them and could feel no sympathy for them. But he was curious to know whether his work during the last few impossible seconds had done what he must have been trying. Mad or not, he had attempted to save them. In doing that, he had destroyed the madness in himself but left himself no chance to test his sanity.

He felt the box begin to slip again and held his breath. But there was no use in that. With its mass, the faint difference any movement of his would make couldn't count.

Isotope R, he thought. It was the answer—that or a mixture containing a high percentage of it. He could have forced his mind through the tortuous process of determining the formula exactly, but he didn't care that much. He wondered what would happen if it was Isotope R—and the answer that came to him sent him screaming through his mind for denial, and finding none.

It had to be Isotope R out there. And if it was, it wouldn't matter whether he died now, was rescued by a miracle, or lived until the inevitable moment when the substance went through its chain of breakdown and came to its end.

Then he revised that. It would matter if a miracle could save him in time. Given time, given consciousness, his mind could complete its search and find the answer—the answer that would end the menace of Isotope R.

But no man out there would find that answer in time. It would have to come from his brain—and his brain would never stand the forces outside that would come rushing in when the box sank.

Already, the box was tipping. It seemed to slip, and to turn. Something gave under it, held, and then gave again. He waited in curiosity, trying to estimate how long it would take. In a few more seconds, he had the pattern worked out. He was almost happy when the box finally slipped exactly as he had expected. It sank, and he was dimly aware that magma was oozing in through the cracks around the lid, but too uninterested to open his eyes on the chance that it would be bright enough to see.

He blackened one corner of his mind, then another. Finally, there was only a tiny spark left, and then he won completely as it flickered out, leaving him unconscious.

chapter 6

"GIVE ME Dr. Blake's residence—Maple 2337," Ferrel said quickly into the phone. The operator looked blank for a second, starting and then checking a purely automatic gesture toward the plugs. "Maple 2337, I said."

"I'm sorry, Dr. Ferrel, I can't give you an outside line. All trunk lines are out of order." There was a constant buzz from the board, but nothing showed in the panel to indicate whether from white inside lights or the red trunk indicators.

"But this is an emergency, operator. I've got to get in touch with Dr. Blake!"

"Sorry, Dr. Ferrel. All trunk lines are out of order." She started to reach for the plug, but Ferrel stopped her.

"Give me Palmer, then—if his line's busy, cut in and I'll take the responsibility."

"All right." She snapped at her switches. "I'm

sorry, emergency call from Dr. Ferrel. Hold the line and I'll reconnect you." Then Palmer's face was on the panel, and this time the man was making no attempt to conceal the expression of worry.

"What is it, Ferrel?"

"I want Blake here—I'm going to need him. The operator says——"

"Yeah." Palmer nodded tightly, cutting in. "I've been trying to get him myself, but his house doesn't answer. Any ideas of where to reach him?"

"You might try the Bluebird or any of the other night clubs around there." Damn, why did this have to be Blake's celebration night? No telling where he could be found by this time.

Palmer was speaking again. "I've already called all the night clubs and restaurants, and he doesn't answer. We're paging the movie houses and theaters now; just a second . . . Nope, he isn't there, Ferrel. Last reports, no response."

"How about sending out a general call over the radio?"

"I'd—I'd like to, Ferrel, but it can't be done." The manager had hesitated for a fraction of a second, but his reply was positive. "Oh, by the way we'll notify your wife you won't be home. Operator! You there? Good, reconnect the Governor!"

There was no sense in arguing into a blank screen, Doc realized. If Palmer wouldn't put through a radio call, he wouldn't, though it had been done once before. "All trunk lines are out of order. . . . We'll notify your wife. . . . Reconnect the Governor!" They weren't even being careful to cover up!

Jenkins' mouth twitched into a grin "So we're cut off. I knew it already; Meyers just got in with more details." He nodded toward the nurse, who was coming out of the dressing room and trying to smooth out

| 63 |

her uniform. Her almost pretty face was more confused than worried.

"I was just leaving the plant, Dr. Ferrel, when I heard my name on the outside speaker. But I had to wait and wait before they'd let me back in. We're actually locked in here! I saw men at all the gates guarding them with revolvers! They were turning back everyone who tried to leave, and wouldn't tell why, even. Just orders that no one was to leave or enter until Mr. Palmer gave his permission. It's like a prison now. Do you suppose . . . Do you know what it's all about?"

"I know just about as much as you do, Meyers, though Palmer said something about carelessness with one of the ports on Three or Four," Ferrel answered her. "Probably just precautionary measures. Anyway, you'll be on double pay. I wouldn't worry too much about it yet."

"Yes, Dr. Ferrel." She nodded and turned back to the front office, but there was no assurance in her look. Doc realized that neither Jenkins nor himself was a picture of confidence at the moment.

"Jenkins," he said when she was gone, "if you know anything I don't, for the love of Mike, out with it! I've never seen anything like this around here."

Jenkins seemed to hesitate. Then he shook himself, and for the first time since he'd been there, used Ferrel's nickname. "Doc, I don't—I know just enough to be less sure than you can be, and I'm scared as hell!"

"Let's see your hands." The subject was almost a monomania with Ferrel, and he knew it, but he also knew it wasn't unjustified. Jenkins' hands came out promptly, and there was no tremble to them. The boy threw up his arm so the loose sleeve slid beyond the elbow, and Ferrel nodded; there was no sweat trickling down from the armpits to reveal a worse case of nerves than showed on the surface. "Good enough, son; I don't care how scared you are—I'm getting that way myself—but with Blake out of reach and the other nurses and attendants gone, I'll need everything you've got."

"Doc?"

"Well?"

"If you'll take my word for it, I can get another nurse here—and a good one, too. They don't come any steadier or any better, and she's not working now. I didn't expect her to—well, anyhow, she'd skin me if I didn't call when we need her. Want her?"

"No trunk lines for outside calls," Doc reminded him. It was the first time he'd seen any real enthusiasm on the boy's face, and however good or bad the nurse was, she'd obviously be of value in bucking up Jenkins' spirits. "Go to it, though, if you can reach her; right now we can probably use any nurse. Sweetheart?"

"Wife." Jenkins started toward the office. "And I don't need an outside line. When I called her to let her know we'd be on the graveyard shift, she said she'd be waiting. So she's sitting in the outside parking lot right now."

"She'd have had a long wait," Doc observed dryly.

Jenkins grinned briefly, and for a second his face was almost boyish. "She expected it. And if you're worried about her ability, she was operating nurse under Bayard at Mayo's; that's what paid my way through medical school!"

The siren was approaching again when Jenkins came back, the little tense lines about his lips still there, but his whole bearing was steadier. He nodded. "I got Palmer, all right, and he okayed having her paged and passing her inside without asking any questions. The switchboard girl has standing orders to route all calls from us through to Palmer before anything else, it seems."

Doc nodded, his ear cocked toward the drone of the siren that drew up and finally ended on a sour wheeze. He felt a sudden relief from tension as he saw Jones hurrying toward the rear entrance; work, even under the pressure of emergency, was always easier than sitting around waiting for trouble. He saw the two stretchers come in, both bearing double loads, and noted that Beel was babbling at the attendant, the driver's usually phlegmatic manner completely gone.

"I'm quitting; I'm through tomorrow! No more watching 'em drag out stiffs for me—not that way. Dunno why I gotta go back, anyhow; it won't do 'em any good to get in further, even if they can. From now on, I'm driving a truck, so help me I am."

Ferrel let him rave on, aware that the man was close to hysteria. He had no time to give Beel now as he saw the red flesh through the visor of one of the armor suits. "Cut off what clothes you can, Jones," he directed. "At least get the shield suits off them. Tannic acid jelly ready, nurse?"

"Ready," Meyers answered. Jenkins was busily helping Jones strip off the heavily armored suits and helmets.

Ferrel kicked on the supersonics again, letting them sterilize the metal suits—there was no time to be finicky about asepsis; the supersonics and ultra-violet tubes were supposed to take care of that, and Ferrel would have to trust them, little as he liked it. Jenkins finished his work, dived back for fresh gloves, with a mere cursory dipping of his hands into antiseptic and rinse. Dodd followed him, while Jones wheeled three of the cases into the middle of the surgery, ready for work; the other had died on the way in.

It was going to be a messy job, obviously. Where

metal from the suits had touched, or come near touching, the flesh had burned—crisped, rather. But that was merely a minor part of it; there was more than ample evidence of major radiation burns, which had probably not stopped at the surface but penetrated through the flesh and bones into the vital interior organs. Doc glanced at Jones questioningly, and the man held up one of the little self-developing strips from an employee badge; it was completely black, showing that the margin of safety had been grossly exceeded.

Much worse, the writhing and spasmodic muscular contractions indicated that radioactive matter had been forced into the flesh and was acting directly on the nerves controlling the motor impulses. Jenkins looked hastily at the twisting body of his case, and his face blanched to a yellowish-white; either it was the first real example of the full possibilities of an atomic accident he'd seen, or he was reading something extra into it. His sick voice seemed unsurprised. "A blast of gamma radiation first. Now it's a beta emitter. It figures!"

His hands clenched, and he threw an involuntary glance in the direction of the converters. Then he seemed to catch himself.

"Curare," he said finally, the word forced out, but level. Meyers handed him the hypodermic and he inserted it, his fingers still steady—more than normally steady, in fact, with that absolute lack of tremor than can come to a living organism under the stress of emergency. Ferrel dropped his eyes back to his own case, both relieved and worried. It was too much of a coincidence that Jenkins had guessed the need for curare so accurately.

From the spread of the muscular convulsions, there could be only one explanation: somehow radioactives had not only worked their way through the air

| 67 |

grills but had been forced through the almost air-tight joints and sputtered directly into the flesh of the men.

A few of the super-heavy isotopes were capable of sending out beta emissions—high-energy electrons —in massive quantities, and this was obviously such a substance. Now the little deposits were driving out such radiation into the nerves, blocking the normal impulses from the brain and spinal column, setting up anarchic orders of their own that made the muscles writhe and jerk, one against the other, without pattern or reason, or any of the normal restraints of the body. It was as if the usual negative feedback controls on the nerves had all gone positive. The closest parallel was that of a man undergoing metrozol shock for schizophrenia, or a severe case of strychnine poisoning.

Doc injected curare carefully, meting out the dosage according to the best estimate he could make, but Jenkins had been acting under pressure and had finished the second injection as Doc looked up from his first. Still, in spite of the rapid spread of the drug, some of the twitching went on.

"Curare," Jenkins repeated, and Doc tensed mentally; he'd still been debating whether to risk the extra dosage. But he made no counter-order, feeling relieved at having the matter taken out of his hands. Jenkins went back to work, pushing up the injections to the absolute limit of safety, and slightly beyond. One of the cases had started a weird hacking moan as his lungs and vocal cords went in and out of synchronization, but it stilled under the drug and in a matter of minutes he lay quiet, breathing with the shallow flaccidity common to curare treatment. The others were still moving slightly, but the violent bone-breaking convulsions had diminished to a spasmodic shudder, similar to a man with a chill.

"God bless the man who synthesized curare,"

Jenkins muttered as he began cleaning away damaged flesh.

Doc could repeat that; with the older, natural product, true standardization and exact dosage had been next to impossible. Too much, and its action on the body was fatal; the patient died from "exhaustion" of his chest muscles in a matter of minutes. Too little was practically useless. Now that the danger of self-injury and fatal exhaustion from wild exertion was over, he could attend to such relatively unimportant things as the agony still going on—curare had no particular effect on the sensory nerves. He injected paramorphine and began cleaning the burned areas and treating them with the standard tannic-acid solution, as well as with antibiotics to eliminate possible infection. Now and then he glanced up at Jenkins.

He had no need to worry, though; the boy's nerves were frozen into an unnatural calm and he worked with a speed Ferrel made no attempt to equal.

Doc gestured, and Dodd handed him the little radiation indicator. He began hunting over the skin, inch by inch, for the almost microscopic bits of matter; there was no hope of finding all now, but the worst deposits could be found and removed.

Later, the nurses could handle the slower process of washing out what was left with versenes and other chemicals, as well as replacing the blood whose cells would be damaged. Fortunately, treatment for even heavy doses of radiation had been well developed for years. They were fortunate also that most of the radiation from the particles here came as beta rays, rather than the more insidious neutrons.

"Jenkins," he asked, "how about I-713's chemical action? Is it basically poisonous to the system?"

"No. Perfectly safe except for radiation. Full quota in the outer electron shell, chemically inert."

That, at least, was a relief. Radiations were bad

enough, but when coupled with metallic poisoning, like the old radium or mercury cases, it was even worse. An inert element would also be less likely to have an affinity for any of the tissues, or to settle in the calcium of the bones. Probably the versenes would flush most of it from the body, and its short half-life would decrease the long hospitalization and suffering of the men. He started for the cabinet where the flushing chemicals were stored, but Jenkins shook his head.

"No good! You can't wash out inert elements with chelating agents."

Doc nodded ruefully to himself. He should have known that himself—he had known it, if he'd stopped worrying long enough to think. So now they'd have to scrape away what they could and let the stuff wear away and be discarded by the body naturally. Fortunately, at least, the half-life was short.

Jenkins joined him on the last patient, replacing Dodd at handing instruments. Doc would have preferred the nurse, who was used to his little signals, but he said nothing, and was surprised to note the efficiency of the boy's cooperation. "How about the breakdown products?" he asked.

"Isotope 713? Harmless enough, mostly, and what isn't harmless isn't concentrated enough to worry about. That is, if it's still I-713. Otherwise——"

Otherwise, Doc finished mentally, the boy meant there'd be no danger from poisoning, at least. Isotope R, with an uncertain degeneration period, turned into Mahler's Isotope, with a complete breakdown in a billionth of a second. He had a fleeting vision of men, filled with a fine dispersion of that, suddenly erupting all over their bodies with a violence that could never be described; Jenkins must have been thinking the same thing. For a second, they stood there, looking at each other silently, but neither chose to speak of it.

Ferrel reached for the probe, Jenkins shrugged, and they went on with their work and their thoughts.

It was a picture impossible to imagine, which they might or might not see; if such an atomic blow-up occurred, what would happen to the Infirmary was problematical. No one knew the exact amount Maicewicz had worked on, except that it was the smallest amount he could make, so there could be no good estimate of the damage. The bodies on the operating tables, the little scraps of removed flesh containing the minute globules of radioactive substance, even the instruments that had come in contact with them, were bombs waiting to explode. Ferrel's own fingers took on some of the steadiness that was frozen in Jenkins, as he went about his work, forcing his mind onto the difficulties at hand.

It might have been minutes or hours later when the last dressing was in place and the three broken bones of the worst case were set. Meyers and Dodd, along with Jones, were taking care of the men, putting them into the little wards, and the two physicians were alone, carefully avoiding each other's eyes, waiting without knowing exactly what they expected.

Outside, a droning chug came to their ears and the thump of something heavy moving over the runways. By common impulse they slipped to the side door and looked away from them. Night had fallen, but the gleaming lights from the big towers around the fence made the plant stand out in glaring detail. They watched the tank moving away, then other buildings cut off their view.

From the direction of the main gate a shrill whistle cut the air and there was a sound of men's voices, though the words were indistinguishable. Sharp, crisp syllables followed, and Jenkins nodded slowly to himself. "Ten'll get you a hundred," he began, "that—— Uh, no use betting. It is."

A squad of men marched into sight from around the corner, making a half-hearted attempt at precision. They were wearing state militia uniforms and each carried a rifle. Under a sergeant's directions, they spread out until each had taken a post before the door of one of the buildings. One started for the Infirmary. Ferrel reached toward the phone to protest to Palmer, but the man went on by toward another building. His face was unshaven and there was something like fear in his expression.

"So that's what Palmer was talking to the Governor about," Ferrel muttered. "No use asking them questions, I suppose; they know less than we do. Come on inside where we can sit down and rest. Wonder what good the militia can do here—unless Palmer's afraid someone inside's going to crack and cause trouble."

Jenkins followed him back to the office and accepted a cigarette automatically as he flopped back into a chair. Doc was discovering just how good it felt to give his muscles and nerves a chance to relax, and realizing that they must have been far longer in the surgery than he had thought. "Care for a drink?"

"Uh—is it safe, Doc? We're apt to be back in there any minute."

Ferrel grinned and nodded. "It won't hurt you —we're just enough on edge and tired for it to be burned up inside for fuel instead of reaching our nerves. Here." It was a generous slug of bourbon he poured for each, enough to send an immediate warmth through them, and to relax their over-strained nerves. "Wonder why Beel hasn't been back long ago?"

"That tank we saw probably explains it; it got too tough for the men to work in just their suits, and they've had to start excavating through the converters with the tanks. If that's the case, whatever they're doing is tough and slow work. And there must be a lot of radiation or heat around if they can't face it in their suits. I was hoping they could break the main port seals into the converter, but it doesn't look like it. Then they could start making plans to damp the action before—— Sue!"

Ferrel looked up to see a girl standing there, already dressed for surgery, and he was not too old for a little glow of appreciation to creep over him. No wonder Jenkins' face lighted up. She was small, but her figure was shaped like that of a taller girl, not in the cute or pert lines usually associated with shorter women, and the serious competence of her expression hid none of the loveliness of her face. Obviously she was several years older than Jenkins, but as he stood up to greet her, her face softened and seemed somehow youthful beside the boy's as she looked up.

"You're Dr. Ferrel?" she asked, turning to the older man. "I'm afraid I'm late. There was some trouble about letting me in at first. So I went directly to prepare before bothering you. And just so you won't be afraid to use me, my credentials are here."

She pulled them from a simple saddle-leather handbag and put them on the table. Ferrel ran through them briefly; she was better than he'd expected. Technically she wasn't a nurse at all, but a doctor of medicine—a so-called nursing doctor. There had been the need for assistants midway between doctor and nurse for years, having the general training and abilities of both, but only in the last decade had the actual course been created and the graduates were still limited in number. He nodded and handed the papers back.

"We can use you, Dr.——"

"Brown—professional name, Dr. Ferrel. And I'm used to being called just Nurse Brown."

Jenkins cut in on the formalities. "Sue, did you hear anything outside about what's going on here?"

"Rumors, but they were wild, and I didn't have a

chance to hear many. Mostly from some of the guards who were beginning to clear out the parking lot. All I know is that they're talking of evacuating the city and everything within fifty miles of here, but it isn't official. One of the guards said they were going to send in Federal troops to declare martial law over the whole section, but there was nothing on the radio."

Jenkins took her off, then, to show her the Infirmary and introduce her to Jones and the two other nurses. Ferrel sat down to wait for the sound of the siren again and tried to imagine what was happening outside in the plant. He attempted to make sense out of the article in the *Weekly Ray,* but finally gave it up; atomic theory had advanced too far since the sketchy studies he'd made, and the symbols were largely without meaning to him. He could work his way through the behavior of the normal elements and the fission of uranium, but the whole process of packing atoms together to form the complicated new isotopes was good only for headaches. He's have to rely on Jenkins, it seemed. In the meantime, what was holding up the litter? He should have heard the warning siren long before.

It wasn't the litter that came in next, however, but a group of five men, two carrying a third, and a fourth supporting the fifth. Jenkins took charge of the carried man, Brown helping him; it was similar to the earlier cases, but without the actual burns from contact with hot metal. Ferrel turned to the men.

"Where's Beel and the litter?" He was inspecting the supported man's leg as he asked, and began work on it without moving the fellow to a table. Apparently a lump of radioactive matter the size of a small pea had been driven half an inch into the flesh below the thigh, and the broken bone was the result of the violent contractions of the man's own muscles under the stimulus of the radiations. It wasn't pretty. Now, however, the strength of the action had apparently burned out the nerves around, and the leg was limp and without feeling; the man lay watching, relaxed on the bench in a half-comatose condition, his lips twisting into a sick grimace, but he did not flinch as the wound was scraped out. Ferrel was working around a small lead shield, his arms covered with heavily leaded gloves, and he dropped the scraps of flesh and isotope into a box of the same metal.

"Beel's out of this world, Doc" one of the others answered when he could tear his eyes off the probing. "He got himself blotto, somehow, and wrecked the litter before he got back. He couldn't take it, watching us grapple them out—and we hadda go in after 'em without a drop to drink!"

Ferrel glanced at him quickly, noticing Jenkins' head jerk around as he did so. "You were getting them out? You mean you didn't come from in there?"

"Hell, no, Doc. Do we look that bad? Them two got it when the stuff decided to spit on 'em. Went clean through their armor. Me, I got me some nice burns, but I ain't complaining. I got a look at a couple of stiffs, so I'm kicking about nothing!"

Ferrel hadn't noticed the three who had traveled under their own power, but he looked now, carefully. They were burned, and badly, by radiations and heat, but the burns were still new enough to give them only a little trouble and probably what they'd just been through had temporarily deadened their awareness of pain, just as a soldier on the battlefield may be wounded and not realize it until the action stops. Anyhow, atomjacks were never noted for being sissies.

"There's almost a quart in the office there on the table," he told them. "One good drink apiece—no more. Then go up front and I'll send Nurse Brown in to fix your burns as well as can be for now." Brown could apply the unguents and administer the serums to counteract normal radiation burns as well as he could, and some division of work seemed necessary. "Any chance of finding any more living men in the converter housing?"

"Maybe. Somebody said the thing let out a groan half a minute before it popped, so most of 'em had a chance to duck into the two safety chambers. Figure on going back there and pushing tanks ourselves unless you say no; about half an hour's work left before we can crack the chambers, I guess, then we'll know."

"Good. And there's no sense sending in every man with a burn, or we'll be flooded here; they can wait, and it looks as if we'll have plenty of serious stuff to care for. Dr. Brown, I guess you're elected to go out with the men; have one of them drive the spare litter Jones will show you. Salve down and inject the burn cases, put the worst ones off duty, and just send in the ones with the jerks. You'll find my emergency kit in the office there. Someone has to be out there to give first aid and sort them out; we haven't room for the whole plant in here."

"Right, Dr. Ferrel." She let Meyers replace her in assisting Jenkins and was gone briefly to come out with his bag. "Come on, you men. I'll hop the litter and dress down your burns on the way. You're appointed driver, mister. Somebody should have reported that Beel person before so the litter would be out there now."

The spokesman for the others upended the glass he'd filled, swallowed, gulped and grinned down at her. "O.K., Doctor, only out there you ain't got time to think—you gotta do. Thanks for the shot, Doc, and I'll tell Hoke you're appointing her out there."

They filed out behind Brown as Jones went to get the second litter and Doc went ahead with the quick-setting plastic cast for the broken leg. Too bad there weren't more of those nursing doctors; he'd have to see Palmer about it after this was over—if Palmer and he were still around. Wonder how the men in the safety chambers, about which he'd completely forgotten, would make out? There were two in each converter housing, designed as an escape for the men in case of accident and supposed to be proof against almost anything. If the men had reached them maybe they were all right; he wouldn't have taken a bet on it, though. With a slight shrug he finished his work and went over to help Jenkins.

The boy nodded down at the still form on the table, already showing signs of extensive scraping and probing. "Quite a lot of spitting clean through the armor," he commented. "Those words gave me a picture of hell boiling out there. Isotope 713 couldn't do that!"

"Umm." Doc was in no mood to quibble on the subject. He caught himself looking at the little box in which the stuff was put after they worked what they could out of the flesh, and jerked his eyes away quickly. Whenever the lid was being dropped a glow could be seen inside. Jenkins always managed to keep his eyes on something else.

If it should turn into Mahler's Isotope, the amount there was large enough already to blow up the whole Infirmary, at least.

chapter 7

PALMER'S INTERCOM clicked softly. "Mayor Walker's on the phone again," Thelma's tired voice announced.

Palmer cursed and swallowed the last of his tasteless sandwich in an unchewed lump. This was the third call from the Mayor since the man had gone back to Kimberly, and Palmer was fed up with the troubles of the town. "Tell him to call back in ten minutes," he answered. "Tell him anything you like. I won't talk to him now."

He should never have agreed to see Walker in the first place. The petition to abolish the bus service out here wasn't that important. If the man hadn't been in Palmer's office when the accident first happened a lot of things could have been handled differently. But the Mayor had got to one of the phones while Palmer had still been trying to find out what had happened, and the Governor had been on the wire before it could be stopped. Now, instead of his own troubles Palmer had the worries of the town and state demanding his time.

He stared down at the tangle of walks below his window. There was nothing to see, since the converters lay on the other side of the building. There was only the sight of a figure in the militia uniform, pacing about under the raw lights, clutching awkwardly at his rifle. Palmer knew there were others all over the place and still more outside the gates. There they might be of some use if the rabble element of the anti-atom crowd proved as edgy as Walker seemed to think, but in here they were only a nuisance.

He glanced at his watch, surprised to see the time. Peters should have reported the latest on the emergency work long before this. He reached for the intercom switch. "Thelma, call out there and find out what's going on!"

"Yes, sir." Her voice sounded worried, and he knew she'd been noticing the time too. "Briggs is on the line."

He picked up the receiver, to see Briggs's tired, ugly face filling the screen. The man nodded. "We've shut down, boss. All we have to do is dump her and test it."

There had been no trouble with the batch at Number Three. It had proceeded exactly as Jorgenson's schedule predicted and Palmer had decided to let it run, since there was no way of knowing what would happen if conversion stopped before completion.

"Good work, Briggs," Palmer told him. "Think you can handle the rest of it?"

Briggs nodded and hung up. His test would be useless for the records, if anyone ever questioned it, since he wasn't able to put a degree after his name. But it would have to do. The foreman knew enough to be trusted. He'd come to National as a working student when the atomic plants were first permitted to give field degrees, but he'd apparently liked being a foreman well enough to stick to it, refusing to go on.

Palmer went out to the outer office, tired of the impersonal speaker. "What about that call?" he asked the girl.

"They don't even answer!"

He almost welcomed the news. He was tired of marking time here, waiting for God knew what word, trying to piece things together from clumsy accounts.

But there'd better be a good reason for the lack of reports or answer.

"All right," he decided. "I'm going out. If anyone calls, handle it if you can; if not, send out a runner."

He took the stairs, not waiting for the elevator. Outside, the guard stared at him suspiciously and started forward, then apparently recognized him and went on pacing uselessly. Palmer headed for the converters, listening to the confusion of human and mechanical sounds and trying to make sense of them. Then he was where he could see for himself.

The magma inside the converter had cracked through the small door to the power-control wing, and it was from there that the injured men had been dragged. The wing was a crumpled wreck of broken walls where the machines had battered their way in, and work there had stopped. Now they were attacking the main entrance, where the great slab of a door had been half-fused shut, while other men worked on the outside walls that separated them from the safety chambers.

But it was a sickening chaos that met his eyes instead of the orderly work he'd expected. Every available light glared down on a tangle of men and machines getting in each other's way, moving about helplessly and generally only making things steadily worse. The main entrance should have been cracked fifteen minutes ago, to let in whatever equipment they could improvise to handle the stuff. But the two bulldozers working on it seemed to be making no progress at all.

He spotted a man he knew helping a red-haired woman he'd never seen, but who seemed to be running some kind of a crude field hospital. He shoved his way through until he could grab the man's arm and pull him around. "Where's Peters? Who's running things here? And why in hell wasn't I notified?"

"Stuff got Peters twenty minutes ago." The man pointed to a figure being lifted on a stretcher onto the litter, the head swathed in bandages. "Hoke's been taking over."

Palmer groaned, though the mess fitted that explanation. Hokusai was one of the best theoretical physicists in the field, but he was a hopeless idiot as a director of others and he made things worse by considering himself almost the exact opposite.

The manager started off at a run, heading for Number Three. He saw that the red working lights were off, indicating that the dumping must be finished, and hit the entrance release, waiting for the thick portal to lift enough for him to slide under. Inside, Briggs and the men were grouped around the heavy box beside the test bench.

"I-713," the foreman reported. "Checks out, and pretty pure, too."

That, at least, was a relief. If they ever got out of this mess, National would need all the pull Morgan could swing, and maybe more. The committee of congressmen had announced hours ago that they were canceling their junket, to return to Washington. Undoubtedly, the double accident had made atomic plants unpopular with them, but he suspected that telegrams demanding action had more to do with the change of plans.

There'd be enough I-713 to start Morgan's vote-getting test going, as soon as any way could be found to ship it out, and that should strengthen the congressman's convictions.

But he simply nodded acknowledgment, without stopping to comment. "Peters is out, Hoke's running the rescue," he told Briggs. "Drop the rest of this and get out there!"

"My God!" Briggs's face showed that he was guessing the mess. He tossed orders over his shoulder to a few of the men, collected the others and went out of the converter on the double. As a foreman, he could displace Hoke with no hard feeling, since he was only doing his job. Palmer would have had to argue longer than it took to get the other man.

By the time the manager was out, Briggs was on top of the improvised stand yelling into the P.A. outfit. Lanes began to be cleared and the bulldozers were coming out, while other men began chasing those too near away. A truck took off as if eternal perdition were hanging on its rear bumper and headed for the supply buildings.

"Get back!" Briggs was shouting. "We'll be burning that door off in three minutes. You guys with the hammers! Spread out, make room for welding cutters. And get the lead out. There are men inside those chambers maybe dying!"

There were other orders, but Palmer relaxed as much as he could, watching the attempt to rescue the men. Now that the crews were organized, they began making progress through the thick concrete-and-steel walls. Even if the main entrance was forced first, it might be impossible to bring the men from the converter chambers through the inside, and the only hope was to breach the walls.

He swore at himself for that. The chambers had been meant to protect men as much from fumes and leaks as anything else, with the idea that those inside could be removed by the same crew that handled the damage. The problem of making them with an entrance to the inside and an exit outside had seemed too difficult, without seriously weakening the restraining strength of the housing. In the future there would have to be a solution!

The pneumatic hammers and electric cutters bit in slowly but steadily, while Briggs called for replacements at regular intervals. Then a shout went up, warning everyone to turn his back. The crew near the main entrance had been attaching a bunch of small cylindrical cans to the door, as fast as they could be moved from the truck. Now they were running back. One of them yanked on a cord.

So they were finally using thermodyne bombs to blast away the main entrance. It couldn't be used on the chambers where the men must be; the heat would have been fatal, probably. But at least they would now have a chance to get the fused main port out of the way and estimate some of the possible trouble inside. Breaching the outer converter walls into the chambers was almost finished, but it would still take longer than it would for the entrance to the converter chamber.

Palmer turned at the last minute, knowing he was far enough away to run little risk from the glaring heat of the superthermite, but taking no chances. That stuff should have been used as soon as it was plain that the door was fused, rather than merely stuck. There was a sudden thump and the ground shook a little. He swung back to see the white-hot material of the door dripping and running in puddles. The whole thing had fallen backward, and now machines were moving up, while men battled to get close enough to hook on and snake it away.

One glance inside was enough to tell that there was no chance of removing the men from the chambers through that. The converter was gone; there were only lumps and heaps of slag to show where it had been. Magma was churning about, beginning to flow out viscously as the door was moved. At Briggs's orders, the remainder of the door was snaked around to form a barrier to cut it off, while others went for blocks to build a roadway for the tanks over it.

Palmer stared at the stuff, watching it churn and spit like nothing he had seen before. This was no normal product of a reaction that had got out of control.

It had to be Isotope R, the forerunner of Mahler's Isotope, the most deadly substance that could be created!

Hoke had come up beside him and was staring into the mess, his wrinkled face frozen in an unbelieving stare. "Bad," he said slowly. "Very bad. We musst try, but I think we are have trouble."

He turned away gasping and holding his hand over his stomach. Palmer started after him, but the little man straightened and smiled sickly. "It iss nothing. Gass, I think. My stomach iss sick, no more."

Palmer's own didn't feel too good. Dan Jorgenson! The man was one of the best engineers in the industry, responsible for more patents than any other, and yet his ego had always made the manager mistrust him. He must have gone over his equations with the intention of proving them right, rather than questioning them.

Then the unfairness of this struck Palmer, and he grimaced at himself. Jorgenson wasn't well liked, but that didn't make him less honest. He'd warned Palmer, and the manager had taken it on his own shoulders, forcing the engineer to rush through an untried process. Now Jorgenson was in one of the chambers, or . . .

He dropped that. The man had to be in a chamber. And they'd better get to him soon. The stuff in there was going to need every bit of skill and knowledge that could be mustered, and it was closer to Jorgenson's field than to Hoke's.

Tanks were beginning to edge into the magma, and he saw that Hoke was putting on armor. But his main concern now was with the men working on the safety chambers. They were beginning to reach the inner section of the north chamber, and he moved to where he could get a better view. He had no business there now—he belonged back in the office—but he couldn't leave until he knew the results.

Then suddenly the workers were drawing back and a power grapple moved up to begin ripping out the sections left of the wall. Armored men were waiting to go in but they weren't needed. As the grapple drew back, a score of men began staggering out of the chamber, some supporting others, but moving on their own feet.

None of them was Jorgenson. The man would have towered over them, and his trick suit should have left him in condition to move by himself if any of them could. Palmer started to head toward the improvised first-aid section, before realizing that the woman there would have her hands full enough without questions.

Briggs solved it for him. A runner came from the medical group toward the platform where the foreman was directing things and shouted up to him. Briggs nodded and reached for the P.A. microphone. "Dr. Brown says they're suffering from some burns and a lot of heat and shock, but they'll be all right!"

It brought a yell from the men, but the cries choked off quickly as they turned back to look at the other chamber. Palmer moved around with them. It had taken longer there for some reason, but they were almost through. Grapples were standing by, waiting for the signal. Palmer edged up until he had a good view of the broken section.

A moment later, the grapples were digging out what was left. But this time there were no men following it out. A trickle of magma oozed out behind it. The light that shot into the chamber showed the door locked firmly, but every figure there was out cold, sprawled on whatever could be found to hold them off the stuff on the floor. Some had used the bodies of others.

Armored men began going in cautiously, trying to clear a path for others to follow with stretchers. Some began working on the wall again, trying to enlarge the opening enough for one of the small tanks. But Palmer didn't wait to see what they would bring out. Even if some of the men were still alive it would be no help to him now. No human being from that chamber would be able to work on the impossible job of checking the wild turmoil going on until long after the action was over. He crossed Jorgenson off his list.

Then as he stared at the stuff in the main converter chamber, he tore up his list, leaving only a question mark and a prayer.

chapter 8

FERREL AND JENKINS were almost finished with the final dressing on the last case when the switchboard girl announced a call. They waited to make the last few touches before answering, then filed into the office together. Brown's face was on the screen, smudged and with a spot of rouge standing out on each cheek. Another smudge appeared as she brushed the auburn hair out of her eyes with the back of her wrist.

"They've cracked the converter safety chambers, Dr. Ferrel. The north one held up perfectly, except for the heat and a little burn, but something happened in the other. Oxygen valve stuck, I guess. Most of the men are unconscious but alive. Magma must have sprayed through the door, because sixteen or seventeen have the jerks, and about a dozen are dead. Some others need more care than I can give; I'm having

Hokusai delegate men to carry those the stretchers won't hold, and they're all piling up on you in a bunch right now!"

Ferrel grunted and nodded. "Could have been worse, I guess. Don't kill yourself out there, Brown."

"Same to you." She blew Jenkins a kiss and snapped off, just as the whine of the litter siren reached their ears.

"Get their armor off, somehow, Jones. Grab anyone else to help you that you can. Curare, Dodd, and keep handing it to me. We'll worry about everything else after Jenkins and I quiet them." This was obviously going to be a mass-production sort of business, not for efficiency, but through sheer necessity. And again, Jenkins with his queer taut steadiness was doing two for the one that Doc could do, his face pale and his eyes almost glazed, but his hands moving endlessly and nervelessly on with his work.

Sometime during the night Jenkins looked up at Meyers and motioned her back. "Go get some sleep, nurse; Miss Dodd can take care of both Dr. Ferrel and myself when we work close together. Your nerves are shot and you need the rest. Dodd, you can call her back in two hours and rest yourself."

"What about you, Doctor?"

"Me . . ." He grinned out of the corner of his mouth, crookedly. "I've got an imagination that won't sleep, and I'm needed here." The sentence ended on a rising inflection that was false to Ferrel's ear, and the older doctor looked at the boy thoughtfully.

Jenkins caught his look. "It's okay, Doc. I'll let you know when I'm going to crack. It was okay to send Meyers back, wasn't it?"

"You were closer to her than I was, so you should know better than I." Technically, the nurses were all directly under his control, but they'd dropped such technicalities long before. Ferrel rubbed the small of his back briefly, then picked up his scalpel again.

A faint gray light was showing in the east, and the wards had overflowed into the waiting room when the last case from the chambers was finished as best he could be. During the night the converter had continued to spit occasionally, even through the tank armor twice, but now there was a temporary lull in the arrival of workers for treatment. Doc sent Jones to fetch breakfast from the cafeteria, then headed into the office, where Jenkins was already slumped down in the old leather chair.

The boy was exhausted almost to the limit from the combined strain of the work and his own suppressed jitters, but he looked up in mild surprise as Ferrel began swabbing his arm. He blinked at the prick of the needle, but made no objections. Doc reached for another disposable hypo and gave himself an injection.

"Just one of those new drugs some drummer sold me on," Ferrel told the younger man. "Something to cut our tension and let us go on."

Jenkins nodded, smiling faintly. "The doctor's curse—too much fatigue and too many drugs at hand. I'm told they used to use morphine—real morphine."

"Quite a few did. I hear there are a few who still do. Anyhow, there isn't as much trouble with it as there was when I was younger, before the counteragent was discovered to kill most of its habit-forming tendency. Even five years ago, before they had that, there were times when morphine was useful, Lord knows, though anyone who used it except as a last resort deserved all the hell he got. A real substitute for sleep would be better, of course. Wish they'd finish up the work they're doing on that fatigue eliminator at Harvard. Amphetamines are too limited. Here, eat that!"

Jenkins grimaced at the breakfast Jones laid out in front of him, but he knew as well as Doc that the food was necessary, and he pulled the plate to him. "What I'd give an eye tooth for, Doc, wouldn't be a substitute—just half an hour of good old-fashioned sleep. Only, damn it, even if I knew I had time, I couldn't do it—not with R out there bubbling away."

The telephone annunciator clipped in before Doc could answer. "Telephone for Dr. Ferrel; emergency! Dr. Brown calling Dr. Ferrel!"

"Ferrel answering!" The phone girl's face popped off the screen and a tired-faced Sue Brown looked out at them. "What is it?"

"It's that little Japanese fellow, Hokusai, who's been running things out here, Dr. Ferrel. I'm bringing him in with an acute case of appendicitis. Prepare surgery!"

Jenkins gagged over the coffee he was trying to swallow, and his choking voice was halfway between disgust and hysterical laughter. "Appendicitis, Doc! My God, what comes next?"

It might have been worse. Brown had coupled in the little freezing unit on the litter and lowered the temperature around the abdomen, both preparing Hokusai for surgery and slowing down the progress of the infection so that the appendix was still unbroken when he was wheeled into the surgery. His seamed Oriental face had a grayish cast under the olive, but he managed a faint grin.

"Very sorry, Dr. Ferrel, to bother you. Very sorry. No ether, pleasse!"

Ferrel grunted. "No need of it, Hoke; we'll use hypothermy, since it's already begun. Over here, Jones. . . . And you might as well go back and sit down, Jenkins."

Brown was washing, and popped out again, ready to assist with the operation. "He had to be tied down, practically, Dr. Ferrel. Insisted that he only needed a little mineral oil and some peppermint for his stomach-ache! Why are intelligent people always the most stupid about these things?"

It was a mystery to Ferrel, too, but seemingly the case. He tested the temperature quickly while the surgery cryotherapy equipment began functioning, found it low enough, and began. Hoke flinched with his eyes as the scalpel touched him, then opened them in mild surprise at feeling no appreciable pain. The complete absence of nerve response with its accompanying freedom from post-operative shock was one of the great advantages of low-temperature work in surgery. Ferrel laid back the flesh, severed the appendix quickly and removed it through the tiny incision. Then, with one of the numerous attachments, he made use of the ingenious mechanical stitcher and stepped back.

"All finished, Hoke, and you're lucky you didn't rupture. Peritonitis isn't funny, even though we can cut down on it with the antibiotics. The ward's full, so's the waiting room, so you'll have to stay on the table for a few hours until we can find a place for you; no pretty nurse, either—until the two other girls get here sometime this morning. I dunno what we'll do about the patients."

"But, Dr. Ferrel, I am hear that now surgery— I should be up already. There iss work I am do."

"You've been hearing that appendectomy patients aren't confined now, eh? Well, that's partly true. Johns-Hopkins began it a long time ago. But for the next hour, while the temperature comes back to normal, you stay put. After that, if you want to move around a little you can; but no going out to the converter. A little exercise probably helps more than it harms, but any strain wouldn't be good."

"But, the danger——"

| 90 |

"Be hanged, Hoke. You couldn't help now, long enough to do any good. Until the stuff in those stitches dissolves away completely in the body fluids, you're to take it easy—and that's two weeks, about."

The little man gave in reluctantly. "Then I think I sleep now. But besst you should call Mr. Palmer at once, pleasse! He musst know I am not there!"

Palmer took the news the hard way, with an unfair but natural tendency to blame Hokusai and Ferrel. "Damn it, Doc, I was hoping he'd get things straightened out somehow. I practically promised the Governor that Hoke could take care of it; he's got one of the best brains in the business. Now this! Well, no help, I guess. He certainly can't do it unless he's in condition to get right into things. Maybe Jorgenson, though, knows enough about it to handle it from a wheel chair, or something. How's he coming along—in shape to be taken out where he can give directions to the foremen?"

"Wait a minute." Ferrel stopped him as quickly as he could. "Jorgenson isn't here. We've got thirty-one men lying around, and he isn't one of them; and if he'd been one of the seventeen dead, you'd know it. I didn't know Jorgenson was working, even."

"He had to be; it was his process! Look, Ferrel, I was distinctly told he'd been taken to you. One of the men reported that he'd seen Jorgenson dumped onto the litter. You'd better check up, and quick. With Hoke only half capable, I've got to have Jorgenson."

"I don't have him, and I'd know him or his suit at the first glance. Your man must have mistaken the big fellow from the south safety chamber for him—but that man had black hair and was wearing an ordinary suit, not a Tomlin. What about the group of men who were only unconscious, or the group outside

| 91 |

the converter? You don't know he was inside when it all happened, do you?"

Palmer wiggled his jaw muscles tensely. "Jorgenson would have reported or been reported fifty times. Every man out there knows I'm looking for him. He's gotta be in your ward."

"He isn't, I tell you! And how about moving some of the fellows here into the city hospital?"

"Tried—hospital must have been tipped off somehow about the radioactives in the flesh, and they refuse to let a man from here be brought in." Palmer was talking with only the surface of his mind, his cheek muscles bobbing as if he were chewing his thoughts and finding them tough. "Jorgenson—now Hoke—and Kellar's been dead for years. Not another man in the whole country that understands this field enough to make a decent guess, even; I get lost on page six myself. Ferrel, could a man in a Tomlin five-shield armor suit make the safety in twenty seconds, do you think, from—say, beside the converter?"

Ferrel considered it rapidly. A Tomlin weighed about three hundred pounds, and Jorgenson was an ox of a man, but only human. "Under the stress of an emergency, it's impossible to guess what a man can do, Palmer, but I don't see how he could work his way half that distance."

"Mmmm, I figured. Could he live then, supposing he wasn't squashed? Those suits are almost radiation-proof—or they're supposed to be, at least. They carry their own air for twenty-four hours, and they're designed like moon suits. They soak up excess carbon-dioxide and moisture in chemical filters. There are no openings of any kind. They're supposed to protect a man inside a converter from almost any kind of accident."

"One chance in a billion, I'd guess; but again, it's darned hard to put any exact limit on what can be

| 92 |

done; miracles keep happening every day. Going to try it?"

"What else can I do? There's no alternative. I'll meet you outside Number Four just as soon as you can make it, and bring everything you need to start working at once. Seconds may count!" Palmer's face slid sideways and up as he was reaching for the button, and Ferrel wasted no time in imitating the motion.

By all logic there wasn't a chance, even in a Tomlin. But until they knew, the effort would have to be made; chances couldn't be taken when a complicated process had gone out of control, with now almost certainty that Isotope R was the result—Palmer was concealing nothing, though he had stated nothing specifically. And obviously, if Hoke couldn't handle it, none of the men at other branches of National Atomics or at the smaller, partially independent plants could make even a half-hearted stab at the job.

It all rested on Jorgenson, then. And Jorgenson must be somewhere under that semi-molten hell that could drive through the tank armor and send men into the Infirmary with bones broken from their own muscular anarchy!

Ferrel's face must have shown his thoughts, judging by Jenkins' startled expression. "Jorgenson's still in there somewhere," he said quickly.

"Jorgenson! But he's the man who———. Good Lord!"

"Exactly. You'll stay here and take care of the jerk cases that may come in; Brown, I'll want you out there again. Bring everything portable we have in case we can't move him in fast enough; get one of the trucks and fit it out and be there with it about twice as fast as you can! I'm grabbing the litter now." He accepted the emergency kit Brown thrust into his hands, dumped a stimulant tablet into his mouth without bothering to wash it down, then was out toward the litter. "Number Four, and hurry!"

Palmer was just jumping off a scooter as they cut around Number Three and in front of the rough fence of rope strung out quite a distance beyond Four. He glanced at Doc, nodded, and dived in through the men grouped around, yelling orders to right and left as he went, and was back at Ferrel's side by the time the litter had stopped.

"Okay, Ferrel, go over there and get into armor as quickly as possible! We're going in there with the tanks, whether we·can or not, and be damned to the quenching for the moment. Briggs, get those things out of there, clean out a roadway as best you can, throw in the big crane again, and we'll need all the men in armor we can get—give them steel rods and get them to probing in there for anything solid and big enough —or small enough—to be a man, five minutes at a stretch; they should be able to stand that. I'll be back pronto!"

Doc noted the confused mixture of tanks and machines of all descriptions clustered around the walls —or what was left of them—of the converter housing, and saw them yanking out everything along one side, leaving an opening where the main housing gate had stood, now ripped out to expose a crane boom rooting out the worst obstructions. Obviously they'd been busy at some kind of attempt at quenching the action, but his knowledge of atomics was too little even to guess at what it was. The equipment set up was being pushed aside by tanks without dismantling, and men were running up into the roped-in section, some already armored, others dragging on part of their armor as they went. With the help of one of the atomjacks, he climbed into a suit himself, wondering what he could do in such a casing if anything needed doing.

Palmer had a suit on before him, though, and was waiting beside one of the tanks. It was squat and heavily armored, its front equipped with both a shovel and a grapple swinging from movable beams. "In here, Doc." Ferrel followed him into the housing of the machine and Palmer grabbed the controls as he pulled on a short-wave headset and began shouting orders through it toward the other tanks that were moving in on their heavy treads. The dull drone of the motor picked up, and the tank began lumbering forward under the manager's direction.

"Haven't run one of these since that show-off at a picnic seven years ago," he complained, as he kicked at the controls and straightened out a developing list to left. "Though I used to be pretty handy when I was plain engineer. Damned static around here almost chokes off the radio, but I guess enough gets through. By the best guess I can make, Jorgenson should have been near the main control panel when it started, and have headed for the south chamber. Half the distance, you figure?"

"Possibly, probably slightly less."

"Yeah! And then the stuff may have tossed him around. But we'll have to try to get there." He barked into the radio again. "Briggs, get those men in suits as close as you can and have them fish with their rods about thirty feet to the left of the pillar that's still up —can they get closer?"

The answer was blurred and pieces missing, but the general idea came across. Palmer frowned. "Okay, if they can't make it, they can't; draw them back out of the reach of the stuff and hold them ready to go in. . . . No, safety be damned. Give me a hookup to the public-address system." He waited until Briggs acknowledged, then leaned forward as if driving himself into his microphone. "I need volunteers! Jorgenson's somewhere in this mess, and the only hope we've got is to locate him. I need damned fools who are crazy enough to risk themselves five minutes apiece in here. Family men or single, I don't care! Any of you idiotic—— Look out, you blamed fool!"

The last was to one of the score or more of men who'd started forward. The lead atomjack was scrambling toward something that looked like a standing position; it toppled, but he managed a leap that carried him to another lump, steadied himself, and began probing through the mess. "Oof! You with the crane —stick it in where you can grab any of the men that pass you, if it'll reach. . . . Good! Doc, I know as well as you that the men have no business in there, even five minutes; but I'll send in a hundred more if it'll find Jorgenson!"

Doc said nothing; he knew there'd probably be a hundred or more fools willing to try and he knew the need of them. The tanks couldn't work their way close enough for any careful investigation of the mixed mass of radioactives, machinery, building, debris and destruction, aside from which they were much too slow in such delicate probing; only men equipped with the long steel poles could do that. As he watched, some of the activity of the magma suddenly caused an eruption, and one of the men tossed up his pole and doubled over before falling. The crane operator shoved the big boom over and made a grab, missed, brought it down again, and came out with the heaving body held by one arm, to run it back along its track and twist it outward beyond Doc's vision.

Even through the walls of the tank and the protection of the suit, heat was pouring in. There was the beginning of a burning sensation near those parts of the armor where the insulation was thinnest. He readjusted himself until those spots no longer pressed on him, noticing that Palmer was trying to get the air conditioner set to its maximum; a control seemed to be stuck, but it finally gave with a thump. Ferrel settled back, trying not to think of what was happening to the men who were trying to worm into the heart of it in nothing but armor; nor did he care to watch what was happening to them. Palmer was trying to inch the machine ahead, but the stuff underneath made any progress difficult. Twice something spat against the tank but did not penetrate.

"Five minutes are up," Ferrel told Palmer. "They'd all better go directly to Dr. Brown, who should be out with the truck now, for immediate treatment."

Palmer nodded and relayed the instructions. "Pick up all you can with the crane and carry them back! Send in a new bunch, Briggs. Damn it, Doc, this can go on all day; it'll take an hour to pry around through this mess right here, and then he's probably somewhere else. The stuff seems to be getting worse in this neighborhood, too, from what accounts I've had before. Wonder if that steel plate could be pushed down?"

He threw in the clutch engaging the motor to the treads and managed to twist through toward the plate. There was a slight slipping of the lugs, then the treads caught and the nose of the tank thrust forward; almost without effort, the fragment of housing toppled from its leaning position and slid forward. The tank growled, fumbled, and slowly climbed onto it and ran forward another twenty feet to its end; the support settled slowly, but something underneath checked it and they were still again. Palmer worked the grapple forward, nosing a big piece of masonry out of the way, and two men reached out with the ends of their poles to begin probing, futilely. Another change of men came out, then another.

Briggs's voice crackled erratically through the phones again. "Palmer, I got a fool here who wants to go out on the end of your beam, if you can swing around so the crane can lift him out to it."

"Start him coming!" Again he began jerking the levers, and the tank buckled and heaved, backed and turned, ran forward, and repeated it all, while the plate that was holding them flopped up and down on its precarious balance.

Doc held his breath and began praying to himself! His admiration for the men who'd go out in that stuff was increasing by leaps and bounds, along with his respect for Palmer's ability.

The crane boom bobbed toward them, and the scoop came running out, but wouldn't quite reach; their own tank was relatively light and mobile compared to the bigger machine, but Palmer already had that pushed to the limit and hanging over the edge of the plate. It still lacked three feet of reaching.

"Damn!" Palmer slapped open the door of the tank, jumped forward on the tread and looked down briefly before coming back inside. "No chance to get closer! Whew! Those men earn their money!"

But the crane operator had his own tricks and was bobbing the boom of his big machine up and down slowly with a motion that set the scoop swinging like a huge pendulum, bringing it gradually closer to the grapple beam. The man had an arm out, and finally caught the beam, swinging out instantly from the scoop that drew backward behind him. He hung suspended for a second, pitching his body around to a better position, then somehow wriggled up onto the end and braced himself with his legs. Doc let his breath out and Palmer inched the tank around to a forward position again. Now the pole of the atomjack could cover the wide territory before them, and he began using it rapidly.

"Win or lose, that man gets anything he wants as a bonus," Palmer muttered. "Uh!"

The pole had located something, and was feeling around to determine size; the man glanced at them and pointed frantically. Doc jumped forward to the windows as Palmer ran out the grapple and began pushing it down into the semi-molten stuff under the pole; there was resistance there but finally the prong of the grapple broke under and struck on something that refused to come up. The manager's hands moved the controls gently, making it tug from side to side; reluctantly, the object gave and moved forward toward them, coming upward until they could make out the general shape. It was definitely no Tomlin suit!

"Lead hopper box! Damn—— Wait. Jorgenson wasn't anybody's fool; when he saw he couldn't make the safety, he might . . . Maybe . . ." Palmer slapped the grapple down again, against the closed lid of the chest, but the hook was too large. Then the man clinging there caught the idea and slid down to the hopper chest, his armored hands grabbing at the lid. He managed to lift a corner of it until the grapple could catch and lift it the rest of the way, and his hands started down, to jerk upward again.

The manager watched his motions, then flipped the box over with the grapple, and pulled it closer to the tank body; magma was running out, but there was a gleam of something else inside.

"Start praying, Doc!" Palmer worked it to the side of the tank and was out through the door again, letting the merciless heat and radiation stream in.

But Ferrel wasn't bothering with that now; he followed, reaching down into the chest to help the other two lift out the body of a huge man in a five-shield Tomlin! Somehow, they wrangled the six-hundred-odd pounds out and up on the treads, then into the housing, barely big enough for all of them. The atomjack pulled himself inside, shut the door, and flopped forward on his face, out cold.

"Never mind him—check Jorgenson!" Palmer's voice was heavy with the reaction from the hunt, but he turned the tank and sent it outward at top speed, regardless of risk. Contrarily, it bucked through the mass more readily than it had crawled in through the cleared section.

Ferrel unscrewed the front plate of the armor on Jorgenson as rapidly as he could, though he knew already that the man was still miraculously alive; corpses don't jerk with force enough to move a three-hundred-pound suit appreciably. A side glance, as they drew beyond the wreck of the converter housing, showed the men already beginning to set up equipment to quell the atomic reaction again, but the armor front plate came loose at last, and he dropped his eyes back without noticing details, to cut out a section of clothing and make the needed injections; curare first, then plasma, aminos, paramorphine, and curare again, though he did not dare inject the quantity that seemed necessary. There was nothing more he could do until they could get the man out of his armor. He turned to the atomjack, who was already sitting up, propped against the driving seat's back.

" 'Snothing much, Doc," the fellow managed. "No jerks, just a few burns and that damned heat! Jorgenson?"

"Alive, at least," Palmer answered, with some relief. The tank stopped, and Ferrel could see Brown running forward from beside a truck. "Get that suit off you, get yourself treated for the burn, and then go up to the office. Maybe we can fix you up with a month's paid vacation in Hawaii or something."

Surprise and doubt registered on the man's face. Then he grinned and shook his head. "If you feel like that, boss, I'd a helluva lot rather have a down-payment on a house big enough for all my kids."

"Then pick yourself a house, and it's yours free and clear. You earned it. Maybe we'll toss in a medal or a bottle of Scotch, too. Here, you fellows give a hand."

Ferrel had the suit ripped off with Brown's assistance, and paused only long enough for one grateful breath of clean, cool air before leading the way toward the truck. As he neared it, Jenkins popped out, directing a group of men to move two loaded stretchers into the litter, and nodding jerkily at Ferrel. "With the truck all equipped we decided to move out here and take care of the damage as it came up. Sue and I rushed them through enough to take care of them until we can find more time, so we could give full attention to Jorgenson. He's still living!"

"By a miracle. Stay out here, Brown, until you've finished with the men from inside, then we'll try to find some rest for you."

The three huskies carrying Jorgenson placed him on the table set up, and began hosing off the bulky armor with versene solution, before ripping it off. They finished, and the truck got under way. Fresh gloves came out of a small sterilizer, and the two doctors fell to work at once, treating the badly burned flesh and trying to locate and remove the worst of the radioactive matter.

"No use," Doc stepped back and shook his head. "It's all over him, probably clear into his bones in places. We'd have to put him through a filter to get it all out!"

Palmer was looking down at the raw mass of flesh with all the layman's sickness at such a sight. "Can you fix him up, Ferrel?"

"We can try, that's all. Only explanation I can give for his being alive at all is that the hopper box must have been pretty well above the stuff until a short time ago—very short—and this stuff didn't work in until it sank. He's practically dehydrated now, apparently, but he couldn't have perspired enough to keep from dying of heat if he'd been under all that for even an hour—insulation or no insulation." There was admiration in Doc's eyes as he looked down at the immense figure of the man. "And he's tough; if he weren't, he'd have killed himself by exhaustion, even confined inside that suit and box, after the jerks set in. He's close to having done so anyway. Until we can find some way of getting that stuff out of him, we don't dare risk getting rid of the curare's effect; that's a time-consuming job in itself. Better give him another saline and glucose intravenous, Jenkins. Then, if we do fix him up, Palmer, I'd say it's a fifty-fifty chance whether or not all this hasn't driven him stark crazy."

The truck had stopped, and the men lifted the stretcher off and carried it inside as Jenkins finished the injection. He went ahead of them, but Doc stopped outside to take Palmer's cigarette for a long drag, and let them go ahead.

"Cheerful!" The manager lighted another from the butt, his shoulders sagging. "I've been trying to think of one man who might possibly be of some help to us, Doc, and there isn't such a person anywhere. I'm sure now, after being in there, that Hoke couldn't do it. Kellar, if he were still alive, could probably pull the answer out of a hat after three looks; he had an instinct and genius for it, the best man the business ever had, even if his tricks did threaten to steal our work from under us and give him the lead. But— well, now there's Jorgenson—either he gets in shape, or else!"

Doc nodded, only half-listening. The cigarette helped but he'd have given a lot at the moment for a cup of good coffee or some of Emma's strong tea. Emma . . .

Jenkins' frantic yell reached them suddenly. "Doc! Jorgenson's dead! He's stopped breathing entirely!"

chapter 9

THROUGH THE night Emma Ferrel had sat before the radio and the television set, alternating between them, hugging her dressing gown about her. She had got up only once, and that was to brew herself a pot of strong tea after she caught herself dozing.

But there was no news on the air. Earlier there had been wild rumors and even an account of a riot at the plant that had forced the Governor to call out the militia. Now there was only the hourly showing of the film in which Mayor Walker assured everyone he'd been out to the plant and that there was nothing to fear. There were appeals for calm and for workers to report as usual. All she had learned since dawn was that the turnpike past the plant was closed "for construction," and that blood was badly needed at the hospital. Blood, she knew, was something they'd need for bad cases of radiation poisoning.

She frowned, trying to remember something that had partly wakened her during the brief time she'd been asleep. It was something about Blake, but she couldn't remember the words, though they were on the edge of her mind.

All she knew for sure was that someone had called to say that Roger would be on the night shift; then later someone else had phoned to say he'd be late because of an emergency operation. They were covering something up and she didn't like it. She had listened to too much talk about the mysterious broken bits of atoms that could come flying out, invisible but deadly as they ripped and mangled the helpless tissues. Sometimes she pictured them as little X-ray "worms" with savage biting teeth, though she knew better.

They had taken her second child before it was born, whatever Roger said. And now they were trying to take her husband.

She tried calling the plant again. There was a long delay, and then the operator told her curtly the line was out of order.

Out of pure habit, she began boiling water for another pot of tea. It was her only source of strength now, somehow. She made it and sat sipping it, unaware until it was finished that she'd forgotten to put milk in it. . . . Why hadn't the paper come? It was long overdue.

She turned the sound up on the television set as one of her favorite local reporters came on. But this morning he wasn't any different from the others. He read the news off from a script, telling everyone that there was nothing to worry about, and giving nothing new.

She could remember hearing almost the same words in the same tone of voice when she was a little girl and her family had a farm on the bank of the Missouri. She had sat on the roof of their house, staring at the water and mud that was ruining all they owned, while a battery radio told them everything was under control, that the river had been stopped, and that boats were picking up all stranded people almost immediately.

Her mother had died of pneumonia and exposure after everything was "under control."

She cut off the radio, vaguely troubled by the sounds from the street. The traffic seemed too thin, and even the cars that did pass sounded wrong. She went to the door, looking for the paper again. It wasn't there, but she saw why the street sounded so quiet; there were no children playing in the yards or on the sidewalks. The street was practically deserted, except for two women who were hurrying along together carrying food packages, with a heavily built man swaggering behind them, frequently looking back over his shoulder. Their voices reached her and she stopped in the door, listening.

". . . her husband couldn't even get near the place. They had these guards, see, with machine guns, chasing everybody back. Wouldn't even listen when he told 'em he had a son inside. Course, like Paul says, it served him right for letting the boy go there in the first place," the older woman was saying.

The second woman started to say something, but the man cut in. "A little more of this and I'm gonna start agreeing with them that says we gotta go up there and close that place down before we all wake up dying of something. God knows what they're doing. Like that guy at the meeting says——"

"Ignorant Hoosiers!" the younger woman broke in. "If them atomjerks had obeyed the law and got out when they was supposed to——"

Emma shut the door, disregarding the hatred and trying to make sense of the words. She'd learned more than she had from the radio, at that. The plant was cut off by guards of some kind and nobody could get in. Either it was dangerous to go near it or the men inside were being protected from people like the woman's husband, or whoever the man was. And it meant that some kind of life and work must still be going on there.

Abruptly, she remembered the half-heard phrase on the radio: "Dr. Blake is wanted at work at once." Nothing more than that. But there couldn't be too many doctors here named Blake; and how many would be wanted "at work"? They had practices or went to hospitals and appointments, not to work. It must mean that Blake was missing!

She reached for the telephone again. There was another long delay before the dial tone went on. The phone rang for minutes but there was no answer. That meant either that Blake had already left or that Roger would still be alone there at the plant! Then she remembered the anniversary. The Blakes didn't always celebrate in the best-behaved way. Something might have happened to them or they might just be refusing to answer their phone. They were capable of anything at times like that.

She limped across the floor, staring from the kitchen into the garage. She'd driven at one time, before they operated on her hip. Maybe not too well, but she'd never had an accident, and several times Roger had ridden with her without saying anything. She even had her driver's license, renewed regularly as proof of her ability. And it wasn't as if Roger had got one of those turbine things. She might be rusty, but with the light traffic . . .

She turned toward the stairs, her mind made up, starting the light under the coffee on her way. She didn't want it, but she'd heard that coffee was a good thing before driving; maybe tea would do as well, but she didn't know. She hurried up the stairs as best she could, grabbing the first skirt and blouse she saw, and pulling out heavy sandals. She skipped stockings and make-up. She almost gave up on the underwear, but the idea left her feeling slimy and she compromised by leaving off the slip. Then she ran a comb through her hair, twisting it into a crude bun, and fastened it hastily with pins.

The coffee was boiling when she came down, but she cooled it off and swallowed it somehow.

She spent several wasted minutes looking for the extra keys before she discovered that Roger had left his keys in the lock, as he did too frequently. She tested things, finding the car started easily and that the shift markers were in the same place. But the gas gauge registered nearly empty. She backed out gingerly, worrying about the fenders. She'd never be able to handle the brake well with her leg, but she could always use the hand brake for any sudden stop. Slowly she moved out onto the street and around the corner. It came as a shock to see that the delicatessen was crowded, but a quick glance showed that canned food seemed to be what people were buying. Beside it, the beauty salon was closed, as was the barbershop further on. The hardware store was open, however, and there was a big fresh sign in the window announcing that guns were on sale.

She found the filling station doing business, but only the owner was there. He filled the tank, but shook his head at the charge plate she found in the glove compartment. "Strictly cash today. Too many people packing up and leaving. Couple dozen like that by here already." Then, as she was counting out the money, he leaned closer. "Want a paper—today's paper?"

He pulled one out from under his coat, showing the date. "Only a buck. Cheap, too. Those soldiers or whatever they were picked up darned near every one that was delivered."

"Mine wasn't, this morning." She considered it, catching a glimpse of the headline, but unable to read it. A dollar seemed like a lot, but . . .

"Maybe yours *was* delivered. They even picked 'em off the porches some places, I hear. Friend at the *Republican* got me a few, though. Want it?"

She nodded, and spread it out on the seat, wondering why the paper had been sent out at all if it was only to be pulled back. The headline drove all other thoughts from her mind:

ATOM PLANT EXPLODES!
Building Demolished, Workers
Held by Force, Hint Mayor Involved.

There was a picture of the plant from the air, looking like a very bad shot made in the early morning, and an arrow that pointed to what was supposed to be the exploded building. She read the story quickly, sick fear inside her. Then anger replaced it. It was all a big guess! They didn't know any more than she did. No wonder the men had picked up the papers. From now on she'd never read it again! She'd got it only for the columns, and they'd been getting worse ever since it joined that chain Roger was always cursing against.

She started the car and headed down the street, throwing the paper out at the first corner. Then she wished she'd burned it or something; a boy dived out to rescue it and a crowd was collecting around him as she drove on.

There was very little traffic. The bars were all doing a good business, but a lot of the other stores were closed or deserted. There were still only a few children, always of the rougher sort, and even the adults seemed fewer than usual, with those who were out huddled into groups. The main street seemed ghostly and there wasn't even a traffic cop on the busy corner.

She passed one street that had been crudely

blocked off, with a packed crowd and a loudspeaker shouting something in anger. The sign indicated it was a Citizens' Protest Rally.

Then she was out of the business section. Now things were quieter again. Few cars passed her, and two of those were loaded with all sorts of equipment and carrying whole families. The big X marks were less frequent, too; she'd been seeing them soaped on some windows, with crude lettering warning all atom-jerks to go home—as if they weren't home, right here in Kimberly!

She drew abreast of a girl who was running along dragging two young children with her, screaming loudly. The girl's face was red with tears. Emma braked down carefully and leaned out. "Want a lift?"

The girl got in with her children and mumbled an address. She stared morosely out of the window. "I'm an atomjack's wife!" she announced finally, defiantly.

"That's all right. I'm Doc's wife," Emma told her. The answer seemed to satisfy the girl; she began trying to quiet the children. She even managed a touch of a smile as she got out and went into an apartment building, first looking up and down to make sure there was no one near. There wasn't a person in sight.

Emma sighed, but it had ceased to bother her. There had been something like it once when she was eight; something she couldn't remember had happened, and men had started riding around in white sheets and pillow cases, while the colored people had stood back staring whenever you met them. Something bad had happened, and kept happening for a while until it all died away. She couldn't recall any details, but she still could feel a touch of the fear—not fear you could fight, but fear of something you didn't know. This was somehow like that. Fear of something unknown was like a fog over everything.

Then she saw the Blake residence and breathed

easier. Their car was parked in front and she managed to work in behind it, hoping she wouldn't get a ticket for being so far out. Then she was ringing the bell— or trying to, since it wouldn't ring. She knocked on the door, getting no answer. There was no better result at the kitchen door, though here the curtain wasn't drawn and she could look inside. There was a mess of bottles and broken glass over everything and a fire was burning under a charred, ruined pot.

She went back to the front, taking off her sandal and banging it against the panel of the door. It made a horrible amount of sound, but nobody answered.

Abruptly, a window went up in a house across the street and a man's voice yelled at her. "You, there! Get away from here! We don't want no trouble around here! You get, you hear. I got a gun and I'll use it."

Other windows were opening. Emma felt her face turning scarlet as she hobbled down the steps and back to her car. The idea of them thinking she wanted trouble! For two cents . . .

Then she sobered enough to know that what they were doing might be a good thing, if there were trouble makers. She got into the car and started it under the suspicious eyes of the neighborhood, moving away faster than she liked. There was still no sign from the Blake house.

Almost without thinking, she headed for the turnpike, turning on the radio and then snapping it off in disgust. Now there were only a few cars and a number of trucks on the road; the trucks all seemed to be filled with men in uniform carrying guns. The road had a closed sign further on, but she went around it, behind one of the trucks, and nobody tried to stop her. She'd learned long before that driving a car with M.D. license plates saved a lot of bother, if you just acted natural about what you were doing.

Then far ahead she saw the top of the plant's big flagpole, with the flag whipping about. At least something was still there.

Now her picture of the little X-ray worms with snapping teeth began to creep into her mind. She tried to pretend that they had all grown toothless, unable to bite and tear at her tissues, but she couldn't convince herself. She felt her hands growing sweaty as they always did near the place. But she drove on, nearing the cut-off to the private road. She'd just have to go in and let them bite. Maybe after a while they wouldn't bother her. They didn't seem to bother Roger.

She'd partly expected the guards who were posted at the cut-off and she had decided on the only way she might get through. If they stopped her she could never make it work. But maybe . . .

She hugged as close as she could to the truck of uniformed men, cranking down a window and pointing to the company symbol on the windshield of the car. "Ferrel. Emergency!" she shouted. They weren't plant men, but more of the uniformed ones, and they might not know whether Ferrel was a man or a woman doctor.

She was past them before they could make up their minds to stop her. She watched in the rear-view mirror, but they weren't following her, at least.

The truck ahead swung off to the side, bumping over the grass-grown land toward the top of a hill, and she saw that the road ended with another blockade at the main gate ahead. The trick would never work here where someone from the plant would be posted. There was no use trying anything. She'd just have to see what happened.

The guard who came out wore the uniform of National, she saw. She tore her eyes off the plant, where all the buildings seemed to stand as usual, except for one of the ugly structures that she'd never liked anyhow. She could feel the little sharp-toothed radiation things waiting for her just inside the gate, but she fought against them, trying to look natural as the guard approached.

"Mrs. Ferrel! You can't go in. Absolute orders. I don't know how you got this far."

"How's my husband?" she asked. She stared at the man, trying to remember the name Roger had called him. Then she had it. "Is he all right, Murphy?"

The man ran a nervous hand around the inside of his cap and shook his head, staring toward the militia work on top of the little hill. "Mrs. Ferrel, are any of us? I dunno. He's in there somewhere, God have mercy on him. You can't go in."

"All right," she agreed. "But I won't go back. I'll drive the car into a tree or something if you send me back. How are your daughter's children, Murphy?" She'd finally sorted him out from among the men who got free medical help from Roger outside the plant.

He stared at her, struggling with himself. Finally he nodded. "If you weren't Doc's wife, I'd kick you all the way back to Kimberly," he said darkly. "But I suppose now I gotta say you've seen too much, so you stay. And don't blame me when it gets rough here. With those militia boys more scared to be standing where they are than of getting the jug for desertion . . . Well, you asked for it. Only don't get out of the car or I'll not be responsible for you."

He swung to one of the other guards. "Bill, park her in the lot back there, if you can squeeze another in."

"Toward the front," she said quietly. "I've got to be where I can get in as soon as the gates are open again."

He threw up his hands and nodded.

She settled back in the car, after the guard had parked it with an amazing amount of swearing, and settled down to watching the corner of the Infirmary she could just see. It hadn't been so hard to get here after all. All it took was a little firmness and some reasoning with Murphy.

chapter 10

DODD WAS working artificial respiration and Jenkins had the oxygen mask in his hands, adjusting it over Jorgenson's face, before Ferrel reached the table. He made a grab for the pulse that had been fluttering weakly enough before, felt it flicker feebly once, pause for about three times normal period, lift feebly again, and then stop completely. "Adrenalin!"

"Already shot it into his heart, Doc!" Jenkins began striking Jorgenson's chest, trying to force the heart to start beating again. His voice was bordering on hysteria, but Palmer was obviously closer to it than Jenkins. The manager thrust himself at Ferrel, his fists clenched.

"Doc, you gotta——"

"Get the hell out of here!" Ferrel's hands suddenly had a life of their own as he grabbed frantically for instruments, ripped bandages off the man's chest, and began working against time, when time had all the advantages. It wasn't surgery—hardly good butchery; the bones that he cut through so ruthlessly with savage strokes of an instrument could never heal smoothly after being so mangled. But he couldn't worry about minor details now.

He tossed back the flap of flesh and ribs that he'd hacked out. "Stop the bleeding, Jenkins!" Then his hands plunged into the chest cavity, somehow finding room around Dodd's and Jenkins', and were suddenly incredibly gentle as they located the heart itself and began working on it, the skilled, exact massage of a man who knew every function of the vital organ. Pressure here, there, relax; pressure again—take it easy, don't rush things! It would do no good to try to set it going as feverishly as his emotions demanded. Pure oxygen was feeding into the lungs and the heart could safely do less work. Hold it steady, one beat a second, sixty a minute.

It had been perhaps half a minute from the time the heart stopped before his massage was circulating blood again; too little time to worry about damage to the brain, the first part to be permanently affected by stoppage of the circulation. Now if the heart could start again by itself within any reasonable time, death would be cheated again. How long? He had no idea. They'd taught him ten minutes when he was studying medicine, then there'd been a case of twenty minutes once, and while he was interning it had been pushed up to a record of slightly over an hour and a half, which still stood; but that was an exceptional case. Jorgenson, praise be, was a normally healthy and vigorous specimen, and he had been in first-class condition, but with the torture of those long hours, the radioactive, narcotic and curare all fighting against him, still one more miracle was needed to keep his life going.

Press, massage, relax; don't hurry it too much. There! For a second, his fingers felt a faint flutter, then again; but it stopped. Still, as long as the organ could show such signs there was hope, unless his fingers grew too tired and he muffed the job before the moment when the heart could be safely trusted by itself.

"Jenkins!"

"Yes, sir!"

"Ever do any heart massage?"

"Practiced it in school, on a model, but never actually. Oh, a dog in dissection class, for five minutes. I—I don't think you'd better trust me, Doc."

"I may have to. If you did it on a dog for five minutes, you can do it on a man. Probably. You know what hangs on it."

Jenkins nodded, the tense nod he'd used earlier. "I know—that's why you can't trust me. I told you I'd let you know when I was going to crack; well, it's damned near here!"

Could a man tell his weakness, if he was about finished? Doc didn't know; he suspected that the boy's own awareness of his nerves would speed up such a break, if anything, but Jenkins was a queer case, taut nerves sticking out all over him, yet a steadiness under fire that few older men could have equaled. If he had to use him, he would. There was no other answer.

Doc's fingers were already feeling stiff—not yet tired, but showing signs of becoming so. Another few minutes, and he'd have to stop. There was the flutter again, one—two—three! Then it stopped. There had to be some other solution to this; it was impossible to keep it up for the length of time probably needed, even if he and Jenkins spelled each other. Only Michel at Mayo's could—— Mayo's! If they could get it here in time, that device he'd seen demonstrated at their last medical convention was the answer.

"Jenkins, call Mayo's—you'll have to get Palmer's okay, I guess—ask for Kubelik, and bring the extension where I can talk to him!"

He could hear Jenkins' voice, level enough at

first, then with a depth of feeling he'd have thought impossible in the boy. Dodd looked at him quickly and managed a grim smile, even as she continued with the respiration; nothing could make her blush, though it should have done so.

The boy jumped back. "No soap, Doc! Palmer can't be located, and that post-mortem misconception at the board won't listen!"

Doc studied his hands in silence, wondering, then gave it up; there'd be no hope of his lasting while he sent out the boy. "Okay, Jenkins, you'll have to take over here, then. Steady does it, come on in slowly, get your fingers over mine. Now, catch the motion? Easy, don't rush things. You'll hold out; you'll have to! You've done better than I had any right to ask for so far, and you don't need to mistrust yourself. There, got it?"

"Got it, Doc. I'll try, but for Pete's sake, whatever you're planning, get back here quick! I'm not lying about cracking! You'd better let Meyers replace Dodd and have Sue called back in here; she's the best nerve tonic I know."

"Call her in then, Dodd." Doc picked up a hypodermic syringe, filled it quickly with water to which a drop of iodine added a brownish-yellow color, and forced his tired old legs into a reasonably rapid trot out of the side door and toward Communications. Maybe the switchboard operator was stubborn but there were ways of handling people.

He hadn't counted on the guard outside the Communications building, though. "Halt!"

"Life or death; I'm a physician."

"Not in here—I got orders." The bayonet's menace apparently wasn't enough; the rifle went up to the man's shoulder, and his chin jutted out with the stubbornness of petty authority and reliance on orders.

"Nobody's sick here. There's plenty of phones elsewhere. You get back, and fast!"

Doc started forward and there was a faint click from the rifle as the safety went off; the darned fool meant what he said. Shrugging, Ferrel stepped back —and brought the hypodermic needle up inconspicuously in line with the guard's face. "Ever see one of these squirt curare? It can reach before your bullet hits!"

"Curare?" The guard's eyes flicked to the needle and doubt came into them. The man frowned. "That's the stuff that kills people on arrows, ain't it?"

"It is—cobra venom, you know. One drop on the outside of your skin and you're dead in ten seconds." Both statements were out-and-out lies, but Doc was counting on the superstitious ignorance of the average man about poisons. "This little needle can spray you with it very nicely, and it may be a fast death, but not a pleasant one. Want to put down the rifle?"

A regular might have shot; but the militiaman was taking no chances. He lowered the rifle gingerly, his eyes on the needle, then kicked the weapon aside at Doc's motion. Ferrel approached, holding the needle out, and the man shrank backward and away, letting him pick up the rifle as he went past to avoid being shot in the back. Lost time! But he knew his way around this little building, at least, and went straight toward the girl at the board.

"Get up!" His voice came from behind her shoulder and she turned to see the rifle in one of his hands, the needle in the other, almost touching her throat. "This is loaded with curare, deadly poison, and too much hangs on getting a call through to bother with physician's oaths right now, young lady. Up! No plugs! That's right; now get over there, out of the cell— there, on your face, cross your hands behind your

| 117 |

back, and grab your ankles—right! Now if you move, you won't move long!"

Those gangster pictures he'd seen were handy at that. She was thoroughly frightened and docile. But perhaps not so much so she might not have bungled his call deliberately. He had to put it through himself. Darn it, the red lights were trunk lines, but which plug——? Try the inside one, it looked more logical; he'd seen it done, but couldn't remember. Now you flip back one of these switches—uh-uh, the other way. The tone came in assuring him he had it right, and he dialed the operator rapidly, his eyes flickering toward the girl lying on the floor, his thoughts on Jenkins and the wasted time running on.

"Operator, this is an emergency. I'm Walnut 7654; I want to put in a long-distance call to Dr. Kubelik, Mayo's Hospital, Rochester, Minnesota. If Kubelik isn't there I'll take anyone else who answers from his department. Speed is essential."

"Very good, sir." Long-distance operators, mercifully, were usually efficient. There were the repeated signals and clicks of relays as she put the call through, the answer from the hospital board, more wasted time, and then a face appeared on the screen; but not that of Kubelik. It was a much younger man.

Ferrel wasted no time in introduction. "I've got an emergency case here where all Hades depends on saving a man, and it can't be done without that machine of Dr. Kubelik's; he knows me, if he's there—I'm Ferrel, met him at the convention, got him to show me how the thing worked."

"Kubelik hasn't come in yet, Dr. Ferrel; I'm his assistant. But if you mean the heart-and-lung exciter, it's already boxed and supposed to leave for Harvard this morning. They've got a rush case out there, and may need it——"

"Not as much as I do."

"I'll have to call—— Wait a minute, Dr. Ferrel, seems I remember your name now. Aren't you the chap with National Atomics?"

Doc nodded. "The same. Now about that machine, if you'll stop the formalities——"

The head on the screen nodded once, instant determination showing, with an underlying expression of something else. "We'll ship it to you at once, Ferrel. Got a field for a plane?"

"Kimberly Airport's about eight miles away. I'll have a truck waiting there. How long?"

"Too long, if you have to transship by truck, Dr. Ferrel. Look, it's already being loaded onto a VTL speedster. Don't you have any place where that can set down?"

With a plane that could take off and land vertically, the situation changed. "There's a square of land south of the Infirmary, and I can have that marked out with flares, I guess." At worst, he could get Jones to improvise some kind of light signal. "That do?"

"Fine. Wait a minute." The face vanished from the screen and there was the sound of dialing, followed by low conversation. Then there was louder and much stronger language, followed by more too distant for Ferrel to follow. The man was back quickly, facing Ferrel.

"Okay, the plane is rerouted to you, and they'll give it all possible rush treatment. They estimate about forty minutes until it reaches you."

It was better than Doc had hoped. He started to express his thanks hastily, already reaching for the plug on the switchboard.

"Wait, Dr. Ferrel!" The younger man checked Doc's cutoff. "Can you use the exciter when you get it? It's tricky work—damned tricky."

"Kubelik gave me quite a demonstration and

| 119 |

I'm used to tricky work. I'll chance it—have to. Too long to rouse Kubelik himself, isn't it?"

"Probably. Okay, I've got the telescript already from the airport. The exciter is on the plane, about to be lifted off. I wish you luck!"

Ferrel nodded his thanks, wondering. Service like that was welcome, but it wasn't the most comforting thing, mentally, to know that the mere mention of National Atomics could cause such an about-face. Rumors, it seemed, were spreading, and in a hurry, in spite of Palmer's best attempts. Good Lord, what was going on here? He'd been too busy for any serious worrying or to realize . . . Well, it had got him the exciter, and for that he should be grateful.

He put through a call to Palmer, hoping the man was back in his office. Luck was with him, for once, and Palmer agreed to okay the arrival of the plane without argument. The manager promised to have flares set up at the landing area and a man assigned to ignite them.

The guard was starting uncertainly off for reinforcements when Doc came out, and he realized that the seemingly endless call must have been over in short order. He tossed the rifle well out of the man's reach and headed back toward the Infirmary at a run, wondering how Jenkins had made out. It had to be all right!

Jenkins wasn't standing over the body of Jorgenson; Brown was there instead, her eyes moist and her face pinched in and white around the nostrils, which stood out at full width. She looked up, shook her head at him as he started forward, and went on working at Jorgenson's heart.

"Jenkins cracked?"

"Nonsense! This is woman's work, Dr. Ferrel, and I took over for him, that's all. You men try to use brute force all your lives and then wonder why a woman can do twice as much delicate work where strong muscles are a nuisance. I chased him out and took over, that's all." But there was a catch in her voice as she said it, and Meyers was looking down entirely too intently at the cycling of the oxygen device.

"Hi, Doc!" It was Blake's voice that broke in. "Get away from there; when this Dr. Brown needs help, I'll be right in there. I've been sleeping like a darned fool all night, from four this morning on. I guess we were really tanked up. We decided to cut the bell and put the phone under a pillow, for some reason. So I didn't hear a darned thing until some idiot came around trying to break in and the neighbors chased her. You go rest."

Ferrel grunted in relief; Blake might have been dead-drunk when he finally got to bed, which would explain his actions with the phone, but his animal virility had soaked it out with no visible sign. The only change was the absence of the usual cocky grin on his face as he moved over beside Brown to test Jorgenson. "Thank the Lord you're here, Blake. How's Jorgenson doing?"

Brown's voice answered in a monotone, words coming in time to the motions of her fingers. "His heart shows signs of coming around once in a while, but it doesn't last. He isn't getting worse, from what I can tell, though."

"Good. If we can keep him going forty minutes more, we can turn all this over to a machine. Where's Jenkins?"

"A machine? Oh, the Kubelik exciter, of course. He was working on it when I was there. We'll keep Jorgenson alive until then anyway, Dr. Ferrel."

"Where's Jenkins?" he repeated sharply, when she stopped with no intention of answering the former question.

Blake pointed toward Ferrel's office, the door of which was now closed. "In there. But lay off him, Doc. I saw the whole thing, and he feels like the devil about it. He's a good kid, but only a kid, and this kind of hell could get any of us."

"I know all that." Doc headed toward the office, as much for a smoke as anything else. The sight of Blake's rested face was somehow an island of reassurance in this sea of fatigue and nerves. "Don't worry, Brown, I'm not planning on dressing him down, so you needn't defend your man so carefully. If was my fault for not listening to him."

Brown's eyes were pathetically grateful in the brief flash she threw him and he felt like a heel for the gruffness that had been his first reaction to Jenkins' absence. If this kept on much longer, though, they'd all be in worse shape than the boy, whose back was toward him as he opened the door. The still, huddled shape did not raise its head from its arm as Ferrel put his hand onto one shoulder, and the voice was muted and distant.

"I cracked, Doc—high, wide and handsome, all over the place. I couldn't take it! Standing there, Jorgenson maybe dying because I couldn't control myself, the whole plant blowing up, all my fault. I kept telling myself I was okay, I'd go on, then I cracked. Screamed like a baby! Dr. Jenkins—*nerve* specialist!"

"Yeah. . . . Here, are you going to drink this, or do I have to hold your blasted nose and pour it down your throat?" It was crude psychology but it worked. Doc handed over the drink, waited for the other to down it and passed a cigarette across before sinking into his own chair. "You warned me, Jenkins, and I risked it on my own responsibility, so nobody's kicking. But I'd like to ask a couple of questions."

"Go ahead—what's the difference?" Jenkins had

obviously recovered a little, judging from the note of defiance that managed to creep into his voice.

"Did you know Brown could handle that kind of work? And did you pull your hands out before she could get hers to replace them?"

"She told me she could. I didn't know before. I dunno about the other; I think . . . Yeah, Doc, she had her hands over mine. But——"

Ferrel nodded, satisfied with his own guess. "I thought so. You didn't crack, as you put it, until your mind knew it was safe to do so, and then you simply passed the work on. By that definition, I'm cracking, too. I'm sitting in here, smoking, talking to you, when out there a man needs attention. The fact that he's getting it from two others, one practically fresh, the other at least a lot better off than we are, doesn't have a thing to do with it, does it?"

"But it wasn't that way, Doc. I'm not asking for grandstand stuff from anybody."

"Nobody's giving it to you, son. All right, you screamed—why not? It didn't hurt anything. I growled at Brown when I came in for the same reason: exhausted over-strained nerves. If I went out there and had to take over from them, I'd probably scream myself, or start biting my tongue. Nerves have to have an outlet; physically it does them no good but there's a psychological need for it." The boy wasn't convinced and Doc sat back in the chair, staring at him thoughtfully. "Ever wonder why I'm here?"

"No, sir."

"Well, you might. Twenty-seven years ago, when I was about your age, there wasn't a surgeon in this country—or the world, for that matter—who had a better reputation than I had for handling difficult operations on the brain. They're still using some of my techniques . . . Yes, I thought you'd remember when the association of names hit you. . . I had a different wife then, Jenkins, and there was a baby coming. Brain tumor—I had to do it, no one else could. I did it, somehow, but I went out of that operating room in a haze, and it was three days later before they'd tell me she'd died; not my fault—I know that now—but I couldn't realize it then.

"So I tried setting up as a general practitioner. No more surgery for me! And because I was a fair diagnostician, which most surgeons aren't, I made a living, at least. Then when this company needed a doctor, I applied for the job and got it; I still had a reputation of sorts. It was a new field, something requiring study and research and damned near every ability of most specialists plus a general practitioner's, so it kept me busy enough to get over my phobia about surgery. Compared to me, you don't know what nerves or cracking means. That little scream was a minor incident."

Jenkins made no comment, but lighted the cigarette he'd been holding. Ferrel relaxed farther back into the chair, knowing that he'd be called if there was any need for his work, and glad to get his mind at least partially off Jorgenson. "It's hard to find a man for this work, Jenkins. It takes too much ability at too many fields, even though it pays well enough. We went through plenty of applicants before we decided on you and I'm not regretting our choice. As a matter of fact, you're better equipped for the job than Blake was. Your record looked as if you'd deliberately tried for this kind of work."

"I did."

"Mmm." That was the one answer Doc had least expected; so far as he knew, no one deliberately tried for a job at Atomics; they usually wound up trying for it after comparing their receipts for a year or so with the salary paid by National. "Then you knew what was needed and picked it up in toto. Mind if I ask why?"

Jenkins shrugged. "Why not? Turnabout's fair play. It's kind of complicated, but the gist of it doesn't take much telling. Dad—my stepfather, that is—had an atomic plant of his own, and a darned good one too, Doc, even if it wasn't as big as National. I was working in it as an engineer when I was fifteen. But we were a little weak on medical radioactive development, so Dad insisted I take up medicine at the university. That's where I met Sue, in her last year. I had money enough to give her a rush then, even though she wasn't around after the one year. She was already holding down a job at Mayo's while I was boning up on medicine. Anyway . . .

"Dad got a big contract on a new process we'd worked out. It took some swinging, but he financed the equipment and started it. . . . My guess is that one of the controls broke through faulty construction; the process itself was right! We'd been over it too often not to know what it would do. But when the estate was cleaned up, I had to go back to medicine full time. Sue supported us, and she had enough pull to swing me an internship at Mayo's. It wasn't atomics, but I figured I'd still use what I learned on that, if I could get on here. Then you hired me."

"National can give a degree in atomics," Doc reminded the boy. The field was still too new to be a standing university course, and there were no better teachers in the business than such men as Palmer, Hokusai and Jorgenson. "They pay a salary while you're learning, too."

"Umm. Takes ten years that way, and the salary's just enough for a single man. No, I'd married Sue with the intention she wouldn't have to work again; well, she did until I finished the internship, but I knew if I got the job here I could support her. As an atomjack, working up to an engineer, the prospects weren't so good. We're saving a little money now and someday maybe I'll get a crack at it. . . . Doc, what's all this about? You babying me out of my fit?"

Ferrel grinned at the boy. "Nothing else, son, though I was curious. And it worked. Feel all right now, don't you?"

"Mostly, except for what's going on out there—I got too much of a look at it from the truck. Oh, I could use some sleep, I guess, but I'm okay again."

"Good." Doc had profited almost as much as Jenkins from the rambling off trail talk, and had managed more rest from it than from nursing his own thoughts. "Suppose we go out and see how they're making out with Jorgenson? What happened to Hoke, come to think of it?"

"Hoke? Oh, he's in my office now, figuring out things with a pencil and paper since we wouldn't let him go back out there. I was wondering——"

"Atomics? Then suppose you go in and talk to him; he's a good guy and he won't give you the brush-off. Nobody else around here apparently suspected this Isotope R business, and you might offer a fresh lead for him. With Blake and the nurses here and the men out of the mess except for the tanks, there's not much you can do to help on my end."

Ferrel felt more at peace with the world than he had since the call from Palmer as he watched Jenkins head off across the surgery toward his office; and the glance that Brown threw, first toward the boy, then back to Doc, didn't make him feel worse. That girl could say more with her eyes than most women with their mouths! He went over toward the operating table, where Blake was now working the heart massage with one of the fresh nurses attending to the respirator that was sighing rhythmically as oxygen was forced into the lungs and sucked out again. The body could exist under such treatment for a while, but they were already reaching the limits that had previously been proved possible.

Blake looked up, his expression worried. "This isn't so good, Doc. He's been sinking in the last few minutes. I was just going to call you. I——"

The last words were drowned out by the bull-throated drone that came dropping down from above them, a sound peculiarly characteristic of the larger VTL airplanes during their vertical descent or takeoff. Ferrel nodded at Brown's questioning glance, but he didn't choose to shout as his hands went around those of Blake and took over the delicate work of stimulating the natural heart action. As Blake withdrew, the sound stopped and Doc motioned him out with his head.

"You'd better go to them and oversee bringing in the apparatus—and grab up any men you see to act as porters—or send Jones for them. The machine is an experimental model and pretty cumbersome; must weigh a couple hundred pounds or more."

"I'll get them myself; Jones is busy."

There was no flutter to Jorgenson's heart under Doc's deft manipulations, though he was exerting every bit of skill he possessed. "How long since there was a sign?"

"About four minutes now. Doc, is there still a chance?"

"Hard to say. Get the machine, though, and we'll hope."

But still the heart refused to respond, though the pressure and manipulation kept the blood circulating and would at least prevent any starving or asphyxiation of the body cells. Carefully, delicately, he brought his mind into his fingers, trying to woo a faint quiver.

Perhaps he did, once, but he couldn't be sure. It all depended on how quickly they could get the machine working now and how long a man could live by manipulation alone. That point was still unsettled.

But there was no question about the fact that the spark of life burned faintly and steadily lower in Jorgenson, while outside the man-made hell went on ticking off the minutes that separated it from becoming Mahler's Isotope. Normally Doc was an agnostic, but now unconsciously his mind slipped back into the simple faith of his childhood, and he heard Brown echoing the prayer that was on his lips. The second hand of the watch before him swung around and around again before he heard the sound of men's feet at the back entrance, and still there was no definite quiver from the heart under his fingers. How much time did he have left, if any, for the difficult and unfamiliar operation required?

He glanced sideways to see that the machine had already been stripped of its protective packing. Blake and a couple of men who must have come in the plane began moving the clumsy-looking piece of apparatus into place beside the body of Jorgenson.

Another side glance at the machine showed the control panel with a seemingly innumerable bunch of induction coils and bundles of wires ending in fine filaments of platinum that would have to be inserted properly to govern the action of Jorgenson's heart and breathing muscles. Everything was carefully coded, yet the complexity was almost terrifying. There was a set of sheets mounted above the console which detailed the coding, and again the number of entries was frightening. All that should have been memorized in advance, with the sheets used only for quick refreshers, but Doc had no time for more than a quick study. And if he made a mistake anywhere, it was at least certain that there would be no chance for a second trial; if his fingers shook or his tired eyes clouded at the wrong instant, there would be no further help for Jorgenson. Jorgenson would be dead!

chapter 11

"TAKE OVER massage, Brown," he ordered, "and keep it up no matter what happens. Good. Dodd, assist me, and hang on to my signals. If it works we can all rest afterward."

He turned toward the machine, his hasty glance showing that the technicians had already plugged it into the electrical outlets. He waved them aside brusquely and kicked on the supersonics and ultraviolet tubes. Keeping the operating theater properly aseptic had become impossible.

"Dr. Ferrel! Wait a——"

One of the men who'd apparently come with the plane to deliver the machine was starting forward. Doc had no time to waste on any last-minute instructions. He swung back to Jorgenson, motioning irritably toward Jones. "Get those men back out of the way. And begin to prepare blood to replace Jorgenson's once this is finished!"

"No. Wait just a minute, Dr. Ferrel!" It was the same man's voice, this time more insistent.

Doc frowned, trying to study the first sheet of coding information. "Blake, give Jones a hand with those men. And if you have any trouble, call in the guards! All right, Brown, that's fine. Ready, Dodd."

Ferrel wondered grimly with that part of his mind that was off by itself whether he could justify his boast to Jenkins of having been one of the world's greatest surgeons; it had been true once, he knew with no need for false modesty, but that was long ago and this was at best a devilish job. He'd hung on with a surge of the old fascination as Kubelik had performed it on a dog at the convention, and his memory for such details was still good, as were his hands. But something else goes into the making of a great surgeon and he wondered if that was still with him.

Then as his fingers made the microscopic little motions needed and Dodd became another pair of hands, he ceased wondering. Whatever it was, he could feel it surging through him and there was a pure joy to it somewhere, over and above the urgency of the work. This was probably the last time he'd ever feel it, and if the operation succeeded, probably it was a thing he could put with the few mental treasures that were still left from his former success. The man on the table ceased to be Jorgenson, the excessively gadgety Infirmary became again the main operating theater of that same Mayo's which had produced Brown and this strange new machine, and his fingers were again those of the Great Ferrel, the miracle boy from Mayo's, who could do the impossible twice before breakfast without turning a hair.

Some of his feeling was devoted to the machine itself. It was hand-built, showing signs of having been torn down and altered repeatedly; there was no decorative cover, no smooth symmetry that would grace later, commercial designs. Massive, ugly, with parts sticking out in haphazard order, it was more like something from an inquisition chamber than a scientist's achievement, but it worked; he'd seen it functioning. In that ugly mass of assorted pieces, little currents were generated and modulated to simulate the normal impulses of the nerves, integrated to make the breathing and circulation fit the needs of the body; there were scanners to place over certain blood vessels, checking the oxygen ratio and the wastes from veins and arteries. It had a brain of sorts, a complex calculator to replace the orders given by a brain that no longer worked or could not drive the proper messages to the organs they should control.

The newspapers had referred to it as a super-pacemaker, but that was nonsense. The pacemaker controlled only the heart, inducing its response. This regulated heart and lungs together, compelling response. A normal pacemaker would have been useless on Jorgenson.

The exciter was a product of the combined genius of medicine and electronics; but wonderful as it was, it was distinctly secondary to the technique Kubelik had evolved for selecting and connecting only those nerves and nerve bundles that were necessary, bringing the almost impossible into the limits of surgical possibility. And now, straining to follow the code Kubelik must know by heart, Ferrel was attempting to duplicate the other man's work!

Brown interrupted, and that interruption in the midst of such an operation indicated clearly the strain she was under. "The heart fluttered a little then, Dr. Ferrel."

Ferrel nodded, untroubled by the interruption. Talk, which bothered some surgeons, was habitual in his own little staff and he always managed to have one part of his mind reserved for that while the rest went on without noticing. "Good. That gives us at least double the leeway I expected."

His hands went on, first with the heart, which was the more pressing danger. Would the machine work, he wondered, in this case? Curare and radioactives, fighting each other, were an odd combination. Yet the machine controlled the nerves close to the vital organ, pounding its message through into the muscles, where the curare had a complicated action that paralyzed the whole nerve, establishing a long block to the control impulses from the brain. Could the nerve impulses from the machine be forced through the short paralyzed passages? Probably—the strength of its signals was controllable. The only proof was in trying.

Brown drew back her hands and stared down uncomprehendingly. "It's beating, Dr. Ferrel! By itself . . . it's beating!"

He nodded again, though the mask concealed his smile. His technique was still not faulty and he had performed the operation correctly after seeing it once on a dog! He was still the Great Ferrel! Then, the ego in him fell back to normal, though the lift remained, and his exultation centered around the more important problem of Jorgenson's living; at least there now seemed a chance, though what the man's condition would be when he revived was still a matter Doc preferred not to consider at the moment.

The problem of attaching the machine to control the breathing muscles was less demanding but more time consuming. Brown proved her worth during the process; she seemed almost able to read his thoughts, to know in advance what he needed, and to have her mind fully synchronized to his fingers. As the lungs finally began moving by themselves, he was expecting it. He nodded in satisfaction and began connecting the sensors that would monitor the needs and control the operation of the machine, which was already adjusted roughly—probably according to the instructions of Kubelik's cooperative assistant.

The remaining detail was soon over. Ferrel nodded to Blake to take over the closing up and final work. He watched until he judged it safe to have the oxygen mask removed from Jorgenson's face, made a few final adjustments to the controls of the machine. Then he stepped back, dropping the habitual sterile mask from his face and pulling off his gloves.

"Congratulations, Dr. Ferrel!" The voice was guttural, strange. "A truly great operation—truly great. I almost stopped you but now I am glad I did not; it was a pleasure to observe you, sir." Ferrel looked up in amazement at the bearded, smiling face of the man who had interrupted him before the operation, and abruptly he realized it was the face of Kubelik himself! He started to mutter words of explanation for not recognizing the surgeon. But Kubelik apparently expected no apology as his huge hand clasped around Doc's.

"I, Kubelik, came, you see; I could not trust another with the machine, and fortunately I was at the airport. Then when you had me shoved aside before I could offer my help, I knew there was no time for arguments. And you seemed so sure, so confident . . . I remained quietly on the sidelines, cursing myself. Now I shall return—since you have no need of me— the wiser for having watched you. . . . No, not a word; not a word from you, sir. Don't destroy your miracle with words. The plane awaits me, I go; but my admiration for you remains forever!"

Ferrel still stood looking down at his hand as the roar of the plane cut in, then at the breathing body with the artery on the neck now pulsing regularly. That was all that was needed; he had been admired by Kubelik, the man who thought all other surgeons were fools and nincompoops. For a second or so longer he treasured it, then shrugged it off.

"Now," he said to the others, as the troubles of the plant fell back on his shoulders, "all we have to do is hope that Jorgenson's brain wasn't injured by the session out there, or by this continued artificially maintained life, and try to get him in condition so he can talk before it's too late. God grant us time! Blake, you know the detail work as well as I do and we can't both work on it. You and the fresh nurses take over, doing the bare minimum needed for the patients scattered around the wards and waiting room. Any new ones?"

"None for some time; I think they've reached a stage where that's over with," Brown said.

"I hope so. Then go round up Jenkins and lie down somewhere. That goes for you and Meyers too, Dodd. Blake, give us three hours if you can, then get us up. There won't be any new developments before then, and we'll save time in the long run by resting. Jorgenson's to get first attention!"

The old leather chair made a fair sort of bed, and Ferrel was too exhausted to benefit as much as he should from sleep of three hours' duration, for that matter, though it was almost imperative he try. Idly, he wondered what Palmer would think of all his safeguards had he known that Kubelik had come into the place so easily and out again. Not that it mattered; it was doubtful whether anyone else would want to come near, let alone inside the plant.

In that, apparently, he was wrong. It was considerably less than the three hours when he was awakened to hear the bull-roar of a VTL plane outside. But sleep clouded his mind too much for curiosity and he started to drop back into his slumber. Then another sound cut in, jerking him out of his drowsiness. It was the sharp sputter of a machine gun from the direction of the gate, a pause and another burst; an eddy of sleep-memory indicated that it had begun before the plane's arrival, so it couldn't be that they were shooting at. More trouble, and though it was none of his business he could not go back to sleep. He got up and went out into the surgery, just as a gnomish little man hopped out from the rear entrance.

The fellow scooted toward Ferrel after one bird-like glance at Blake, his words spilling out with a jerky self-importance that should have been funny, but missed it by a small margin; under the surface, sincerity still managed to show. "Dr. Ferrel? Uh—Dr. Kubelik—Mayo's, you know—he reported you were shorthanded; stacking patients in the other rooms. We volunteered for duty—me, four other doctors, nine nurses. Probably should have checked with you, but couldn't get a phone through. Took the liberty of coming through directly, fast as we could get all our stuff together and get it loaded onto the plane. We're digging it out now."

Ferrel glanced through a rear window and saw that the loading ramp of the plane was down, with men and equipment beginning to come off it. He kicked himself mentally for not asking for help when he'd put through the call for the exciter; but he'd been used to working with his own little staff so long that the ready response of his profession to emergencies had been almost forgotten.

"You know that you're taking chances coming here? Then in that case I'm grateful to you and Kubelik. We've got about forty patients here, all of whom should have considerable attention, though I frankly doubt whether there's room for you to work."

The man hitched his thumb backward jerkily. "Don't worry about that. Kubelik goes the limit when he arranges things. Everything we need with us, practically all the hospital's atomic equipment; though maybe you'll have to piece us out there. Even a field hospital tent, portable wards for every patient you have. Want relief in here, or would you rather have us simply move out the patients to the tent, leave this end to you? Oh, Kubelik sent his regards. Amazing of him!"

Kubelik, it seemed, had a tangible idea of regards, however dramatically he was inclined to express them; with him directing the volunteer force, the wonder was that the whole staff and equipment hadn't been moved down. "Better leave this end," Ferrel decided. "Those in the wards will probably be better off in your tent, as well as the men now in the waiting room; we're equipped beautifully for all emergency work, but not used to keeping the patients here any length of time, so our accommodations that way are rough. Dr. Blake will show you around and help you get organized in the routine we use here. He'll get help for you in erecting the tent, too. By the way, did you hear the commotion by the entrance as you were landing?"

"We did, indeed. We saw it, too—bunch of men in some kind of uniform shooting a machine gun; hitting the ground, though. Bunch of other people running back away from it, shaking their fists, looked like. We were expecting a dose of the same, maybe; didn't notice us, though."

Blake snorted in half-amusement. "You probably would have got it if our manager hadn't forgotten to give orders covering the air approach; they must figure that's an official route." He beckoned the little doctor after him, then turned his head to address Brown over his shoulder. "Show Doc the results while I'm gone, honey."

Ferrel forgot his new recruits and swung back to the girl. "Bad?"

She made no comment, but picked up a lead shield and placed it over Jorgenson's chest so that it cut off all radiation from the lower part of his body, then placed the radiation indicator close to the man's throat. Doc looked once; no more was needed. It was obvious that Blake had already done his best to remove the radioactive from all parts of the body needed for speech, in the hope that they might strap down the others and block them off with local anesthetics; then the curare could have been counteracted long enough for such information as was needed. Equally obviously, he'd failed. There was no sense in going through the job of neutralizing the drug's block only to have him under the control of the radioactive still present. The stuff was too finely dispersed for surgical removal. Now what? He had no answer.

Jenkins' lean-sinewed hand took the indicator from him for inspection. The boy was already frowning as Doc looked up in faint surprise, and his face made no change. He nodded slowly. "Yeah. I figured as much. That was a beautiful piece of work you did, too. Too bad. I was watching from the door and you almost convinced me he'd be all right, the way you handled it. But . . . So we have to make out without him; and Hoke and Palmer haven't even cooked up a lead that's worth a good test. Want to come into my office, Doc? There's nothing we can do here."

Ferrel followed Jenkins into the little office off the now-empty waiting room; the men from the hospital had worked rapidly, it seemed. "So, you haven't been sleeping, I take it? Where's Hokusai now?"

"Out there with Palmer; he promised to behave, if that'll comfort you. . . . Nice guy, Hoke; I'd forgotten what it felt like to talk to an atomic engineer without being laughed at. Palmer, too. I wish . . ." There was a brief light in the boy's face and the first glow of normal human pride Doc had seen in him. Then he shrugged, and it vanished back into his taut cheeks and reddened eyes. "We cooked up the wildest kind of a scheme, but it isn't so hot."

Hoke's voice came out of the doorway, as the little man came in and sat down carefully in one of the three chairs. "No, not so hot! It iss fail already. Jorgensson?"

"Out, no hope there! What happened?"

Hoke spread his arms, his eyes almost closing. "Nothing. We knew it could never work, not so? Missster Palmer, he iss come soon here, then we make planss again. I am think now besst we should move from here. Palmer, I—mostly, we are theoreticians; and excuse, you alsso, doctor. Jorgensson wass the production man. No Jorgennsson, no—ah—soap!"

Mentally, Ferrel agreed about the moving and soon! But he could see Palmer's point of view; to give up the fight was against the grain somehow. And besides, once the blow-up happened, with the resultant damage to an unknown area, the pressure groups would have a field day. They might even force the congressional committee to go further than the current bill to move all atomic plants out into some barren section where workers couldn't be persuaded to follow; the crackpot fringe that had been shouting for the end of all tinkering with atomics might sweep into complete control. If by some streak of luck Palmer could save the plant with no greater loss of life and property than already existed, there would be enough proof that atomics could be handled safely to win over the saner elements, and the benefits from the products National made would again outweigh all risks. But . . .

"Just what will happen if it all goes off?" he asked.

Jenkins shrugged, biting at his inner lip as he went over a sheaf of papers on the desk covered with the scrawling symbols of atomics. "Anybody's guess. Suppose three million tons of the army's new explosive were to explode in a billionth of a second. Normally, you know, compared to atomics, that stuff burns like any fire, slowly and quietly, giving its gases plenty of time to get out of the way in an orderly fashion.

Figure it one way, with this all going off together, and the stuff could drill a hole that'd split open the whole continent from Hudson Bay to the Gulf of Mexico, and leave a lovely sea where the Middle West is now. Figure it another, and it might only kill off everything within fifty miles of here. Somewhere in between is the chance we count on. This isn't a hydrogen bomb, you know."

Doc winced. He'd been picturing the plant going up in the air violently, with maybe a few buildings somewhere near it, but nothing like this. It had been purely a local affair in his mind but this didn't sound like one. No wonder Jenkins was in that state of suppressed jitters; it wasn't too much imagination but too much cold, hard knowledge that was worrying him. Ferrel looked at their faces as they bent over the symbols once more, tracing out point by point their calculations in the hope of finding one overlooked loophole, then decided to leave them alone.

The whole problem was hopeless without Jorgenson, it seemed, and Jorgenson was his responsibility; if the plant went, it was squarely on the senior physician's shoulders. But there was no apparent solution. If it would help, he could cut it down to a direct path from brain to speaking organs, strap down the body and block off all nerves below the neck, using an artificial larynx instead of the normal breathing through vocal cords. But the indicator showed the futility of it; the orders could never get through from the brain with the amount of radioactive still present throwing them off track—even granted that the brain itself was not affected, which was doubtful.

Fortunately for Jorgenson the stuff was all finely dispersed around the head, with no concentration at any one place that was unquestionably destructive to his mind; but the good fortune was also the trouble, since it could not be removed by any means known to medical practice. Even so simple a thing as letting the man read the questions and spell out the answers by winking an eyelid as they pointed to the alphabet was hopeless.

Nerves! Jorgenson had his blocked out, but Ferrel wondered if the rest of them weren't in as bad a state. Probably somewhere well within their grasp there was a solution that was being held back because the nerves of everyone in the plant were blocked by fear and pressure that defeated its own purpose. Jenkins, Palmer, Hokusai—under purely theoretical conditions, any one of them might spot the answer to the problem, but the sheer necessity of finding it could be the thing that hid it. The same might be true with the problem of Jorgenson's treatment. Yet, though he tried to relax and let his mind stray idly around the loose ends and seemingly disconnected knowledge he had, it returned incessantly to the need for doing something, and doing it now!

Ferrel heard weary footsteps behind him and turned to see Palmer coming from the front entrance. The man had no business walking into the surgery, but such minor rules had gone by the board hours before.

"Jorgenson?" Palmer's conversation began with the same question in the usual tone, and he read the answer from Doc's face with a look that indicated it was no news. "Hoke and that Jenkins kid still in there?"

Doc nodded, and plodded behind him toward Jenkins' office; he was useless to them but there was still the idea that in filling his mind with other things some little factor he had overlooked might have a chance to come forth. Also, curiosity still worked on him, demanding to know what was happening. He flopped into the third chair and Palmer squatted down on the edge of the table.

"Know a good spiritualist, Jenkins?" the manager

asked. "Because if you do, I'm about ready to try calling back Kellar's ghost. The Steinmetz of atomics —so he had to die before this Isotope R came up, and leave us without even a good guess at how long we've got to crack the problem. Hey, what's the matter?"

Jenkins' face had tensed and his body straightened back tautly in his chair, but he shook his head, the corner of his mouth twitching wryly. "Nothing. Nerves, I guess. Hoke and I dug out some things that give an indication on how long this runs, though. We still don't know exactly, but from observations out there and the general theory before, it looks like something between six and thirty hours left; probably ten's closer to being correct!"

"Can't be much longer. It's driving the men back right now! Even the tanks can't get in where they can do the most good, and we're using the shielding around Number Three as a headquarters for the men; in another half hour, maybe they won't be able to stay that near the thing. Radiation indicators won't register any more, and it's spitting all over the place almost constantly. Heat's terrific; it's gone up to around three hundred centigrade and sticks right there now, but that's enough to warm up Three, even."

Doc looked up. "Number Three?"

"Yeah. Nothing happened to that batch; it ran through and came out I-713 right on schedule, hours ago." Palmer reached for a cigarette, realized he had one in his mouth and slammed the package back on the table. "Significant data, Doc; if we get out of this, we'll figure out just what caused the change in Four— if we get out! Any chance of making those variable factors work, Hoke?"

Hokusai shook his head, and again Jenkins answered from the notes. "Not a chance. Sure, theoretically, at least, R should have a period varying between twelve and sixty hours before turning into

| 141 |

Mahler's Isotope, depending on what chains or sub-chains of reactions if goes through; they all look equally good and probably are all going on in there now, depending on what's around to soak up neutrons or let them roam, the concentration and amount of R together, and even high or low temperatures that change their activity somewhat. It's one of the variable reactions, no question about that."

"The spitting iss prove that," Hoke supplemented.

"Sure. But there's too much of it together and we can't break it down fine enough to reach any safety point where it won't toss energy around like rain. The minute one particle manages to make itself into Mahler's, it'll crash through with energy enough to blast the next over the hump and into the same thing instantly and that passes it on to the next at about light speed! If we *could* get it juggled around so some would go off first, other atoms a little later and so on, fine. . . . Only we can't do it unless we can be sure of isolating every blob bigger than a tenth of a gram from every other one! And if we start breaking it down into reasonably small pieces we're likely to have one strike on the short transformation subchain and go off at any time; pure chance gave us a concentration to begin with that eliminated the shorter chains, but we can't break it down into small lots and those into smaller lots and so on. Too much risk!"

Ferrel had known vaguely that there were such things as variables but the theory behind them was too new and too complex for him; he'd learned what little he knew when the simpler radioactives proceeded normally from radium to lead, as an example, with a definite, fixed half-life, instead of the super-heavy atoms they now used that could jump through several different paths, yet end up the same. He'd had it explained to him, but the complexity of the extra electron shells was made worse by references to packed shells;

the engineers talked about doubled nuclei, meson chains and a host of other things and then turned around and denied that they really meant any of them! He'd thought once he was getting somewhere when he heard them discussing fractionating bonds, only to find that they considered each bond—whatever it was —in quantum terms, and hence indivisible! Hoke and Jenkins managed to make all previous discussions he'd heard sound like kindergarten stuff.

It was over his head, and he started to get up and go back to Jorgenson.

Palmer's words stopped him. "I knew it, of course, but I hoped maybe I was wrong. Then—we evacuate! No use fooling ourselves any longer. I'll call the Governor and try to get him to clear the country around; Hoke, you can tell the men to get the hell out of here! All we ever had was the counteracting isotope to hope on and no chance of getting enough of that. There was no sense in making I-631 in thousand-pound batches before. Well . . ."

He reached for the phone but Ferrel cut in. "What about the men in the wards? They're loaded with the stuff, most of them with more than a gram apiece dispersed through them. They're in the same class with the converter, maybe, but we can't just pull out and leave them!"

Silence hit them, to be broken by Jenkins' hushed whisper. "My God! What damned fools we are. I-631 under discussion for hours, and I never thought of it. Now you two throw the connection in my face and I still almost miss it!"

"I-631? But there iss not enough. Maybe twenty-five pound, maybe less. Three and a half dayss to make more. The little we have would be no good, Dr. Jenkinss. We forget that already." Hoke struck a match to a piece of paper, shook one drop of ink onto it and watched it continue burning for a second before putting it out. "So. A drop of water for stop a foresst fire. No!"

"Wrong, Hoke. A drop to short a switch that'll turn on the real stream—maybe. Look, Doc, I-631's an isotope that reacts atomically with R—we've checked on that already. It simply gets together with the stuff and the two break down into non-radioactive elements and a little heat. It's like a lot of other such atomic reactions but it isn't the violent kind. They simply swap parts in a friendly way and open up to simpler atoms that are stable. We have a few pounds on hand, can't make enough in time to help with Number Four, but we do have enough to treat every man in the wards, *including Jorgenson!*"

"How much heat?" Doc snapped out of his lethargy into the detailed thought of a good physician. "In atomics you may call it a little; but would it be small enough in the human body?"

Hokusai and Palmer were practically riding the pencil as Jenkins figured. "Say five grams of the stuff in Jorgenson, to be on the safe side, less in the others. Time for reactions . . . Here's the total heat produced and the probable time taken by the reaction in the body. The stuff's water-soluble in the chloride we have of it, so there's no trouble dispersing it. What do you make of it, Doc?"

"Fifteen to eighteen degrees temperature rise at a rough estimate. Uh!"

"Too much! Jorgenson couldn't stand ten degrees right now!" Jenkins frowned down at his figures, tapping nervously with his hand.

Doc shook his head. "Not too much! We can drop his whole body temperature first in the hypothermy bath down to eighty degrees, then let it rise to a hundred, if necessary, and still be safe. Thank the Lord, there's equipment enough. If they'll rip out the refrigerating units in the cafeteria and improvise baths, the volunteers out in the tent can start on the other men while we handle Jorgenson. At least that way we can get the men all out even if we don't save the plant!"

Palmer stared at them in confusion before his face galvanized into resolution. "Refrigerating units —volunteers—tent? What—— Okay, Doc, what do you want?" He reached for the telephone and began giving orders for the available I-631 to be sent to the surgery, for men to rip out the cafeteria cooling equipment and for such other things as Doc requested. Jenkins had already gone to instruct the medical staff in the field tent, but was back in the surgery before Doc reached it with Palmer and Hokusai at his heels.

"Blake's taking over out there," Jenkins announced. "Says if you want Dodd, Meyers, Jones, or Sue, they're sleeping."

"No need. Get over there out of the way, if you must watch," Ferrel instructed the two engineers as he and Jenkins began attaching the freezing units and bath to the bed where Jorgenson lay. "Prepare his blood for it, Jenkins; we'll force it down as low as we can to be on the safe side. And we'll have to keep tabs on the temperature fall and regulate his heart and breathing to what it would be normally under those conditions. For all I know, Kubelik may have built in compensations somewhere in that machine, but I don't know about them. Anyhow, they're not under the control of his body now."

"And pray," Jenkins added. He grabbed the small box out of the messenger's hand before the man was fully inside the door and began preparing a solution, weighing out the whitish powder and measuring water carefully, but with the speed that was automatic to him under tension. "Doc, if this doesn't work—if Jorgenson's crazy or something—you'll have another case of insanity on your hands. One more false hope would finish me."

"Not one more case; four! We're all in the same boat. Temperature's falling nicely; I'm rushing it a little bit but it's safe enough. Down to ninety-six now." The remote-reading thermometer inserted into Jorgenson's rectum was one intended for cryotherapy work, capable of rapid response, instead of the normal fever thermometer. Slowly, with agonizing reluctance, the little needle on the dial moved over, down to ninety, then on. Doc kept his eyes glued to it, slowing the pulse and breath to the proper speed. He lost track of the number of times he sent Palmer back out of the way, and finally gave up.

Waiting, he wondered how those outside in the field hospital were doing. Still they had ample time to arrange their makeshift cooling apparatus and treat the men in groups—ten hours probably; and hypothermy was a standard thing now. Jorgenson was the only real rush case. Almost imperceptibly to Doc, but speedily by normal standards, the temperature continued to fall. Finally it reached seventy-eight.

"Ready, Jenkins, make the injection. That enough?"

"No. I figure it's almost enough but we'll have to go slow to balance out properly. Too much of this stuff would be almost as bad as the other. Gauge going up, Doc?"

It was, much more rapidly than Ferrel liked. As the injection coursed through the blood vessels and dispersed out to the fine deposits of radioactive, the needle began climbing past eighty, to ninety and up. It stopped at ninety-four and slowly began falling as the cooling bath absorbed heat from the cells of the body. The radioactivity meter still registered the presence of Isotope R, though much more faintly.

The next shot was small, and a smaller one followed. "Almost," Ferrel commented. "Next one should about do the trick."

Using partial injections, there had been need for less drop in temperature than they had given Jorgenson but there was small loss to that. Finally, when the last minute bit of the I-631 solution had entered the man's veins and done its work, Doc nodded. "No sign of activity left. He's up to ninety-five, now that I've cut off the refrigeration, and he'll pick up the little extra temperature in a hurry. By the time we can counteract the curare, he'll be ready. That'll take about thirty minutes, Palmer."

The manager nodded, watching them dismantling the hypothermy equipment and going through the routine of canceling out the curare. It was always a the work had been done already by the normal body slower job than treatment with the drug but part of processes and the rest was a simple, standard procedure. Fortunately the paramorphine would be nearly worn off; that would have been a longer and much harder problem to eliminate.

"Telephone for Mr. Palmer. Calling Mr. Palmer. Send Mr. Palmer to the telephone." The operator's words lacked the usual artificial exactness, and were only a nervous sing-song. It was getting her, and she wasn't bothered by excess imagination normally. "Mr. Palmer is wanted on the telephone."

"Palmer." The manager picked up an instrument at hand; it was not equipped with vision and there was no indication of who the caller was. But Ferrel could see what little hope had appeared at the prospect of Jorgenson's revival disappearing. "Check! Move out of there and prepare to evacuate but keep quiet about that until you hear further orders! Tell the men Jorgenson's about out of it so they won't lack for something to talk about."

He swung back to them. "No use, Doc, I'm

afraid. We're already too late. The stuff's stepped it up again and they're having to move out of Number Three now. I'll wait on Jorgenson, but even if he's all right and knows the answer we probably can't get in to use it!"

chapter 12

PALMER WAS heading past the Administration building toward Briggs and the crew working on Number Four but he stopped himself abruptly. The sight of his observing them without any more answer than they had was the last thing that would help. Briggs was capable of doing everything that they could do now anyhow. Even from a distance it was easy to see that there wasn't much anyone could do, but get out of the stuff's way. Men were no longer going anywhere near it.

Anything they could find as an answer—from Jorgenson or on their own—would be useless unless it could be done in heavy tanks and at a distance. If there had been enough I-631, of course, they could spray it over the magma. But there wasn't.

He turned back reluctantly, passing a group of men lugging up shields to be added to the light tractors and tanks. It was beginning to get them, finally. Up to now they'd been willing to accept it as a challenge and to leave the solution to him. But now they were giving up. He'd already had a report on a small group who had tried to crash out through the freight loading yard and another who had apparently been trying to force the main gate. So far the guards had no serious trouble. But if the men here ever really wanted out, one of the tanks would clear the way in a hurry. There'd be riots and general hell in plenty, though, if the men broke into separate groups with some remaining loyal while others tried to break away. Maybe there'd be chaos anyhow. There was a limit to how much tension a man could keep enduring without losing his self-control.

Palmer could feel his own nerves going. The proof of it was that he kept thinking of more and more fantastic schemes, though the logical part of his mind knew that nearly any good solution was the simplest way rather than the most complicated. Transmutation hadn't been solved by magical rigmarole but by knowledge and the simple accumulation of enough of the right elements in the right place. The mechanisms of the converter were simpler than those of the old cyclotron, though they could put out neutrons by the pound and mesons in almost any concentration.

He headed for his office, half-thinking that he might get a quick shower there. If he could relax he might do no more but he'd be in a better position to get work out of others.

He knew his mistake as soon as he stepped inside and saw Thelma's face. All the calls that had been piling up were still waiting for him, only stalled off by her tricks.

"What is it?" he asked bitterly.

"Mayor Walker right now," she told him. "He's the worst."

Palmer took the call in his office, reaching for the bottle under his desk as he did so. It wasn't the equal of a shower but something was needed to keep him going. "All right, Walker," he said. "You're first in line but there are plenty more. What gives?"

He was still cursing the luck that had placed Walker in his office at the moment the mess started. But at least the man was now doing his best to stick to the point and make it brief as he outlined the situation.

Kimberly had finally started to get out of hand. Palmer felt reasonably sure that Guilden hadn't been behind the blatantly false headlines or the bootlegging of copies after the issue was supposedly confiscated under the Governor's emergency orders; it bore the mark of a real fanatic and Guilden wasn't that far gone from his publishing standards. But it didn't matter. The confiscation had convinced the fools that the story was true and the fact that there were no real details merely encouraged them to read what they liked into the bootlegged copies. The mob gatherings were doing the rest. So far no real violence had occurred but the level of fear couldn't be whipped much higher without exploding in all directions, though aimed at the plant.

Palmer cut Walker short. "There's nothing I can do, Walker. And maybe nothing any of us will care about tomorrow. We've about given up!"

The man's face whitened, grew sick and then amazingly firmed into itself again. He took a deep breath, grimaced and nodded. "I suppose we'll get it when you do, eh? Yeah. Well, will it make any difference what happens here, Palmer?"

"I don't know. It might help with that slim chance we have."

"All right." Walker was suddenly commander of his forces and himself again. "If it's that way we'll keep them in line somehow. Let me know if there's anything at all we can do."

He hung up.

It proved what Palmer had been sure of all along. Given enough truth about his situation, a man could face almost anything. But when the attack came in the dark and he had no idea what he was fighting, he broke and went crazy. The whole cover-up insisted on by the Governor had been a mistake from the start. In the minor emergency matters of normal politics it probably made sense, but not on anything at this level.

But it hadn't been the fault of politicians only. It had started with the plants themselves. They'd given up on trying to explain the facts to the people—tough, almost indigestible facts couched in abstruse mathematics, of course; they hadn't faced up to the fact that some way could always be found to make anything understandable, given time. Instead of hiring the best minds to find the way, they'd made the secrets even more esoteric. And when trouble came they'd been forced to try to conceal it and depend on trickery. Morgan's proposal might work, but not forever. In the long run the only way to fight the bill was to bring everything out in the open.

Then he grinned bitterly at himself. He'd told Walker the facts but he hadn't admitted them to himself yet. He was still figuring on the miracle that would save them.

"Congressman Morgan on the phone," Thelma announced.

Palmer started in surprise. Damn it, Morgan had no kicks coming. He'd even found a way to get the shipment sent out on time—all the stuff from the successful conversion—using the militia and the minimum of faking the purpose of the shipment. It should be almost ready for use by now.

But Morgan made no reference to that. "Palmer," he said without preliminaries "what would happen if a hydrogen bomb were dropped on the plant right now?"

"You'd have a lot of dead men," Palmer answered. He stared at the face on the screen, trying to read it and finding it deadly serious.

"I don't mean the personnel—there'd be time to evacuate them," Morgan amended.

Palmer grinned bitterly. "I didn't mean plant personnel, either. I mean anything up to half of the United States!"

It would mean that, too. Once the energy of the fusioning hydrogen hit near the mass of Isotope R out there, the energy level would be lifted to a high-enough point to blast it all straight into Mahler's Isotope. Any energy the bomb couldn't supply on first contact would be derived from the explosion of the part that had switched over and the whole mass would be raw energy, along with assorted atomic fragments, in almost literally no time.

Morgan grunted. "That's what I guessed. I can figure out a little of that—enough to scare me, at least. But I haven't had time to check up with the experts here. Are you sure of it?"

"Hoke figured it out a long time ago, he tells me —Matsuura Hokusai, you've heard of him," Palmer explained. "The stuff we have out there triggers off with about one-tenth the energy it takes to trigger the hydrogen reaction—and it yields about six times as much energy for its mass! Though it's the speed of the stuff that does most of the damage—hydrogen is slow burning, by comparison. Why?"

Morgan stopped to mop his forehead with a kerchief that was already damp, as if he'd been running.

"Because that's the bright idea that they've come up with here, just now. They've about got the President talked into it, too." He paused, as if trying to believe it himself. "They mean to give you until tomorrow morning to get your men out of there and then to come in with small fusion bombs and give it hell. They've figured that they can control it so it won't hit Kimberly too hard. And I can't convince them of anything. I'm only in on the discussions on sufferance. I'd be out on my ear if they knew I leaked it to you."

It was the simple brute-force type of solution that would appeal to men who were used to dealing with normal material problems. Wipe a thing out completely and you could stop worrying about it. Spray enough DDT into a room and there would be no bedbugs; then you could worry about getting rid of the poisonous deposits of DDT later. Only in this case they were dealing with something that wouldn't accept such solutions. This was dangerously close to the borderline between matter and energy, as it was, and material solutions didn't wholly apply. It would solve the problem of R, all right; but there'd be no human beings around afterward close enough to take care of the aftereffects.

"What can I do?" Palmer asked.

"Give me the name of the best man I can get to talk to them in a hurry."

"Morgenstern from M.I.T.," Palmer answered. "Or if you need someone even faster, grab Hazelton from the NACC. He should be able to convince them."

The congressman snorted into the phone. "You don't know, Palmer. You think facts can sell anything but you're wrong. They *can't* believe that their most brilliant idea of all is totally useless. And they can't pick up the rudiments of science in half an hour. They're still thinking in analogies—fight fire with fire, fight atoms with atoms. Hell, Hazelton has been arguing with them for years on everything related to atomics and they've never yet believed him. I'll try him, but don't expect much from it."

Palmer swung to face the windows as he thought it over. Morgan wasn't acting now, obviously. The man was risking what was worth as much to him as the plant was to Palmer. And he was as much of an expert on politics as Hokusai was on theoretical atomics. When he swung back, the manager's decision had been made.

He'd been tearing up all the other rules he'd lived by. He might as well destroy the last one.

"All right," he said. "Tell them to relax. They won't need their bombs, because we've found a way to quench it already. Jorgenson, the man who discovered the process, was in the converter when it all happened. He had instruments on the converter at the exact second it blew up. And he lived through it, in a Tomlin suit, until we could get to him. Now he has recovered enough to outline a way of checking the reaction and my men are putting it into operation right now. Will that help you?"

Morgan nodded as he considered it. "Maybe it will. Especially that stuff about his being inside when it blew and living through it. It's a bigger lie than I'd have thought of but it fits the pattern of stuff they'll swallow. It should get us an extension of time, at least. But God help us both if they ever find out."

He hung up, and Palmer headed for the door before the intercom could call him back. After such conversations he could almost look forward to the news Hoke would have for him, bad as he knew it must be.

chapter 13

FERREL STARED down at Jorgenson, then at the small screen on the exciter which showed interpretations of the man's vital processes. He shook his head doubtfully.

"We could probably disconnect him now. But despite his apparent physical recuperation, I think he'd better stay on the exciter for at least twenty-four hours more." Then he grimaced. "I made a mess of his chest! Healing is going to be a long, slow process, though Blake did his best. The ribs should knit well enough, but he'll never take a pretty X-ray from now on. Well, it won't much matter if he's still sane."

Jenkins stared down at the huge body, his face tense. "Doc, he's got to be sane!"

"He's been through more hell than any normal human being could take." Doc shook his head again. "Right now, his condition is better than we had a right to expect, but there's no way of knowing how much damage has been done. Don't count on too much help from him."

"We have to count on it, Doc. If Hoke and Palmer find that things out there are what it sounds like, we'll have to come up with a better solution than any of us can find. There's an answer somewhere; there has to be. But we won't find it in time without Jorgenson."

"Ummm. Seems to me you've been having ideas

yourself, son. You've been right so far, and if Jorgenson's out of things . . ." Doc finished his inspection and flopped down on a bench, knowing that all they could do was wait for the drugs to work on Jorgenson and bring him around. Now that he relaxed the control over himself, exhaustion hit down with full force; his fingers were uncertain as he pulled off his gloves. "Anyhow, we'll know in another five minutes or so."

"And Heaven help us, Doc, if it's up to me. I've always had a flair for atomic theory; I grew up on it. But he's the production man who's been working at it week in and week out, and it's his process, to boot. . . . There they are now! All right for them to come back here?"

But Hokusai and Palmer were waiting for no permission. At the moment Jorgenson was the nerve center of the plant, drawing them back, and they stalked over to stare down at him, then sat where they could be sure of missing no sign of returning consciousness. Palmer picked up the conversation where he'd dropped it, addressing his remarks to both Hokusai and Jenkins.

"Damn that Link-Stevens postulate! Time after time it fails, until you figure there's nothing to it; then this! It's black magic, not science, and if I get out I'll find some fool with more courage than sense to discover why. Hoke, are you positive it's the *theta* chain? There isn't one chance in ten thousand of that happening, you know. It's unstable, hard to start, tends to revert to the simpler ones at the first chance."

Hokusai spread his hands, lifted one heavy eyelid at Jenkins questioningly, then nodded. The boy's voice was dull, almost uninterested. "That's what I thought it had to be, Palmer. None of the others throw off that much energy at this stage, the way you described conditions out there. Probably the last thing we tried to quench it set it up in that pattern and it's

| 156 |

in a concentration just right to keep it going. We figured ten hours was the best chance, so it had to pick the six-hour short chain."

"Yeah." Palmer was pacing up and down nervously again, his eyes swinging toward Jorgenson from whatever direction he moved. "And in six hours maybe all the population around here can be evacuated, maybe not, but we'll have to try it. Doc, I can't even wait for Jorgenson now! I've got to get the Governor started at once!"

"They've been known to practice lynch law, even in recent years," Ferrel reminded him grimly. He'd seen the result of one such case of mob violence when he was practicing privately and he knew that people remain pretty much the same year after year; they'd move, but first they'd demand a sacrifice. "Better get the men out of here first, Palmer, and my advice is to get *yourself* a good long distance off; I heard some of the trouble at the gate, but that won't be anything compared to what an evacuation order will do."

Palmer grunted. "Doc, you might not believe it, but I don't give a continental about what happens to me or the plant right now."

"Or to the men? Put a mob in here hunting your blood and the men will be on your side, because they know it wasn't your fault and they've seen you out there taking chances yourself. That mob won't be too choosy about its targets, either, once it gets worked up, and you'll have a nice vicious brawl all over the place. Besides, Jorgenson's practically ready."

A few more minutes would make no difference in the evacuation, and Doc had no desire to think of his partially crippled wife going through the hell evacuation would be; she'd probably refuse to go until he returned. His eyes fell on the box Jenkins was playing with nervously, and he stalled for time. "I thought you said it was risky to break the stuff down into small particles, Jenkins. But that box contains the stuff in various sizes, including one big piece we scraped out, along with the contaminated instruments. Why hasn't it exploded?"

Jenkins' hand jerked up from it as if burned and he backed away a step before checking himself. Then he was across the room toward the I-631 and back, pouring the white powder over everything in the box in a jerky frenzy. Hokusai's eyes had snapped fully open and he was slopping water to fill up the remaining space and keep the I-631 in contact with everything else. Almost at once, in spite of the low relative energy release, it sent up a white cloud of steam faster than the air conditioner could clear the room; but that soon faded down and disappeared.

Hokusai wiped his forehead slowly. "The suits—armor of the men?"

"Sent 'em back to the converter and had them dumped into the stuff to be safe long ago," Jenkins answered. "But I forgot the box, like a fool. Ugh! Either blind chance saved us, or else the stuff spit out was all one kind, some reasonably long chain I don't know nor care right——"

"S'ot! Nnuh . . . Whmah nahh?"

"Jorgenson!" They swung from the end of the room like one man, but Jenkins was the first to reach the table. Jorgenson's eyes were open and rolling in a semi-orderly manner, his hands moving sluggishly. The boy hovered over his face, his own practically glowing with the intensity behind it. "Jorgenson, can you understand what I'm saying?"

"Uh." The eyes ceased moving and centered on Jenkins. One hand came up to his throat, clutching it, and he tried unsuccessfully to lift himself with the other, but the after-effects of what he'd been through seemed to have left him in a state of partial paralysis.

Ferrel had hardly dared to hope that the man

could be rational, and his relief was tinged with doubt. He pushed Palmer away and shook his head. "No, stay back. Let the boy handle it; he knows enough to avoid a shock to the man now, and you don't. This can't be rushed too much."

"I—uh . . . Young Jenkins? You gotta righ'. Been thinkin'—wrong 'bout ever'thing!" Somewhere in Jorgenson's huge frame, an untapped reserve of energy and will still seemed to exist. He began trying to sit up, his eyes on Jenkins, his hands still catching at the reluctant throat that refused to cooperate.

Jenkins restrained him quietly, moving the thin bundle of cords from the exciter out of the reach of the huge hands. "Take it easy, Mal. You'll be all right, but you've got to relax. Don't strain yourself."

Jorgenson seemed to nod, and his efforts ceased. But he still clutched his throat, as if to loosen the words that would not come. He took a deeper breath, unconsciously overriding the exciter signals. This time, words came again, blurry and uncertain, but somehow made understandable by the determination of the man.

"Y'r dad tol' me——"

"Dad's dead, Mal. Now——"

" 'Sright. 'N y'r grown up. 'Bout twelve years old when we . . . The plant——!"

"Easy, Mal." Jenkins' voice managed to sound casual, though his hands under the table were white where they clenched together. "Listen and don't try to say anything until I finish. The plant's all right, but we've got to have your help. Here's what happened."

Ferrel could make little sense of the cryptic sentences that followed, though he gathered that they were some form of engineering shorthand; apparently, from Hokusai's approving nod, they summed up the situation briefly but fully, and Jorgenson listened attentively until the account was finished, his eyes fastened on the boy.

"Helluva mess. Gotta think. Yuh tried——" His throat seemed to refuse to work further, and he began to twist his head, as if to loosen something. Jenkins placed a hand on the man's forehead to quiet him. Jorgenson relaxed again. He rested for a moment before making a further attempt.

"Uh—need—ugh! Damn throat! Yuh—uh—urrgh!"

"Got it?"

"Uh!" The tone was affirmative, unquestionably, but the clutching hands around his neck told their own story. The temporary burst of energy he'd forced was exhausted and he couldn't get through with the answer. He lay there breathing heavily and struggling, then relaxed after a few more half-whispered words, none intelligently articulated.

Palmer clutched at Ferrel's sleeve. "Doc, isn't there anything you can do?"

"Try." He metered out a minute quantity of drug doubtfully, felt Jorgenson's pulse, and decided on half that amount. "Not much hope, though; that man's been through hell and it wasn't good for him to be forced around in the first place. Carry it too far and he'll be delirious if he does talk. Anyway, I suspect it's partly his speech centers as well as the throat."

But Jorgenson began a slight rally almost instantly, trying again, then apparently drawing himself together for a final attempt. When they came, the words spilled out harshly in forced clearness, but without inflection.

"First . . . variable . . . at . . . twelve . . . water . . . stop." His eyes, centered on Jenkins, closed, and he relaxed again, this time no longer fighting off the inevitable unconsciousness.

Hokusai, Palmer and Jenkins were staring back

and forth at one another questioningly. The little Japanese shook his head negatively at first, frowned and repeated it, to be imitated almost exactly by the manager. "Delirious ravings!"

"The great white hope, Jorgenson!" Jenkins' shoulders dropped and the blood drained from his face, leaving it ghastly with fatigue and despair. "Oh, damn it, Doc, stop staring at me! I can't pull a miracle out of a hat!"

Doc hadn't realized that he was staring but he made no effort to change it. "Maybe not, but you happen to have the most active imagination here, when you stop abusing it to scare yourself. Well, you're on the spot now and I'm still giving odds on you. Want to bet, Hoke?"

It was an utterly stupid thing and Doc knew it; but somewhere during the long hours together he'd picked up a queer respect for the boy and a dependence on the nervousness that wasn't fear but closer akin to the reaction of a rear-running thoroughbred on the home stretch. Hoke was too slow and methodical and Palmer had been too concerned with outside worries to give anywhere nearly full attention to the single most urgent phase of the problem; that left only Jenkins, hampered by his lack of self-confidence.

Hoke gave no sign that he caught the meaning of Doc's heavy wink, but he lifted his eyebrows faintly. "No, I think I am not bet. Dr. Jenkinss, I am to be command!"

Palmer looked briefly at the boy, whose face mirrored incredulous confusion, but he had neither Ferrel's ignorance of atomic technique nor Hokusai's fatalism. With a final glance at the unconscious Jorgenson, he started across the room toward the phone. "You men play if you like. I'm starting evacuation immediately!"

"Wait!" Jenkins was shaking himself, physically

as well as mentally. "Hold it, Palmer! Thanks, Doc. You knocked me out of my blue funk, made me remember something that happened a long time ago. I think I know what Jorgenson was trying to tell us. And maybe it's the answer. It has to be—nothing else can save us at this stage of the game!"

"Give me the Governor, operator." Palmer had heard, but he went ahead with the phone call. "Jorgenson didn't tell us anything. He wasn't able to. And if you've got some wild idea, forget it! This is no time to play hunches; at least not until after we get the people out. I'll admit you're a darned clever amateur, but you're no atomicist!"

"And if we get the men out, it's too late—there'll be no one left in here to do the work!" Jenkins' hand snapped out and jerked the receiver of the plug-in telephone from Palmer's hand. "Cancel the call, operator; it won't be necessary. Palmer, you've got to listen to me; you can't clear the whole middle of the continent and you can't depend on the explosion to limit itself to less ground. It's a gamble, but you're risking fifty million people against a mere hundred thousand. Give me a chance!"

"I'll give you exactly one minute to convince me, Jenkins, and it had better be good! Maybe the blow-up won't hit beyond the fifty-mile limit!"

"Maybe. And I can't explain in a minute." The boy scowled tensely. "Okay, you've been belly-aching about a man named Kellar being dead. If he were here would you take a chance on him? Or on a man who'd worked under him on everything he tried?"

"Absolutely, but you're not Kellar. And I happen to know he was a lone wolf; didn't hire outside engineers after Jorgenson had a squabble with him and came here." Palmer reached for the phone. "It won't wash, Jenkins."

Jenkins' hand clamped down on the instrument,

jerking it out of reach. "I wasn't *outside* help, Palmer. When Jorgenson was afraid to run one of the things off and quit, I was twelve; three years later things got too tight for Dad to handle alone but he decided he might as well keep it in the family, so he started me in. I'm Kellar's stepson!"

Pieces clicked together in Doc's head then, and he kicked himself mentally for not having seen the obvious before. "That why Jorgenson knew you, then? I thought that was funny. It checks, Palmer."

For a split second the manager hesitated uncertainly. Then he shrugged and gave in. "Okay. I'm a fool to trust you, Jenkins, but it's too late for anything else, I guess. I never forgot that I was gambling with the locality against half the continent. What do you want?"

"Men—construction men, mostly, and a few volunteers for dirty work. I want all the blowers, exhaust equipment, tubing, booster blowers, and everything ripped from the other three converters and connected as close to Number Four as you can get. Put them up some way so they can be shoved in over the stuff by crane—I don't care how; the shop men will know better than I do. You've got sort of a river running off behind the plant; get everyone within a few miles of it out of there and connect the blower outlets down to it. Where does it end, anyway—some kind of a swamp?"

"About two miles farther down, yes; we didn't bother keeping the drainage system going since the land meant nothing to us and the swamps made as good a dumping ground as anything else." When the plant had first used the little river as an outlet for their waste products, there had been so much trouble that National had been forced to take over all adjacent land and quiet the owners' fears of the atomic activity in cold cash. Since then it had gone to weeds and rabbits, mostly. "Everyone within a few miles is out, anyway, except a few fishers or tramps who don't know we use it. I'll have the militia sent in to scare them out."

"Good. Ideal, in fact, since the swamps will hold stuff longer in there where the current's slow. Now, what about the super-thermite stuff you were producing last year? Any around?"

"Not much in the plant. But we've got tons of it at the warehouse, still waiting for the army's requisition. That's pretty hot stuff to handle, though. Know much about it?"

"Enough to know it's what I want." Jenkins indicated the copy of the *Weekly Ray* still lying where he'd dropped it, and Doc remembered skimming through the nontechnical part of the description. The super-thermite was made up of two super-heavy atoms, kept separate. By itself neither was particularly important or active but together they reacted with each other atomically to release a tremendous amount of raw heat and comparatively little unwanted radiation. "It's the most concentrated source of heat available, and that's what I'm going to need. How's it stored? How do you set it off?"

"Stored in ten-pound cans. Some of them have trip wires, some electrical connections, some fragile partitions that break with shock, starting the action. Hoke can explain it—it's his baby." Palmer reached for the phone. "Anything else? Then get out and get busy! The men will be ready for you when you get there! I'll be out myself as soon as I can put through your orders."

Doc watched them go out, to be followed in short order by the manager, and was alone in the Infirmary with Jorgenson and his own thoughts. They weren't pleasant; he was both too far outside the inner circle to know what was going on and too much mixed up in it not to know the dangers. Now he could have used some work. . . .

He grunted in disgust at himself and dug out the blood sample of the ringer. It was no great effort to prepare it and to set up the microscope. Then he was studying the cells. There wasn't much question. The excess white count and large number of juvenile cells were typical. Everything indicated chronic myelogenous leukemia. If the woman didn't receive treatment soon, she'd be dead in months, at most.

That meant that Palmer had no worry there— and that Doc again had nothing to do. He wriggled down in the leather chair, making the mistake of trying to force sleep, while his mind chased out after every sound that came in from outside. There were the drones of crane and tank motors coming to life, the shouts of hurried orders and above all the jarring rhythm of pneumatic hammers on metal, each sound suggesting some possibility to him without adding to his knowledge. The *Decameron* was boring, the whiskey tasted raw and rancid, and solitaire wasn't worth the trouble of cheating.

Finally he gave up and turned out to the field hospital tent. Jorgenson would be better off out there under the care of the staff from Mayo's, and perhaps he could make himself useful. As he passed through the rear entrance, he heard the sound of a number of helicopters coming over with heavy loads and looked up as they began settling over the edge of the buildings. From somewhere a group of men came running forward and disappeared in the direction of the freighters. He wondered whether any of those men would be forced back into the stuff out there to return filled with radioactive; though it didn't matter so much now that the isotope could be eliminated without surgery.

Blake met him at the entrance of the field tent, obviously well satisfied with his duty of bossing and instructing the others. "Scram, Doc. You aren't needed here, and you have to get some rest. Don't want you added to the casualties. What's the latest dope from the powwow front?"

"Jorgenson didn't come through, but the kid had an idea and they're out there working on it." Doc tried to sound more hopeful than he felt. "I was thinking you might as well bring Jorgenson in here; he's still unconscious, but there doesn't seem to be anything to worry about. Where's Brown? She'll probably want to know what's up, if she isn't asleep."

"Asleep when the kid isn't? Uh-unh. Mother complex, has to worry about him." Blake grinned. "She got a look at him running out with Hoke tagging at his heels, and hiked out after him, so she probably knows everything now. Wish Anne'd chase me that way just once—Jenkins, the wonder boy! Well, it's out of my line; I don't intend to start worrying until they pass out the order. Okay, Doc, I'll have Jorgenson out here in a couple of minutes, so you grab yourself a cot and get some shut-eye."

Doc grunted, looking curiously at the refinements and well-equipped interior of the field tent. "I've already prescribed that, Blake, but the patient can't seem to take it. I think I'll hunt up Brown, so give me a call over the public speaker if anything turns up."

He headed toward the center of action, knowing that he'd been wanting to do it all along but hadn't been sure of not being a nuisance. Well if Brown could look on, there was no reason why he couldn't. He passed the machine shop, noting the excited flurry of activity going on, and went past Number Two, where other men were busily ripping out long sections of big piping and various other devices. There was a rope fence barring his way, well beyond Number

Three, and he followed along the edge, looking for Palmer or Brown.

She saw him first. "Hi, Dr. Ferrel, over here in the truck. I thought you'd be coming soon. From up here we can get a look over the heads of all these other people and we won't be trampled on." She stuck down a hand to help him up and smiled faintly as he disregarded it and mounted more briskly than his muscles wanted to. He wasn't so old that a girl had to help him yet.

"Know what's going on?" he asked, sinking down onto the plank across the truck body, facing out across the men below toward the converter. There seemed to be a dozen different centers of activity, all crossing each other in complete confusion, and the general pattern was meaningless.

"No more than you do. I haven't seen my husband, though Mr. Palmer took time enough to chase me here out of the way."

Doc centered his attention on the copters, unloading, rising and coming in with more loads, and he guessed that those boxes must contain the little thermodyne bombs. It was the one thing he could understand and consequently the least interesting. Other men were assembling the big sections of piping he'd seen before, connecting them up in almost endless order, while some of the tanks hooked on and snaked them off in the direction of the small river that ran off beyond the plant.

"Those must be the exhaust blowers, I guess," he told Brown, pointing them out. "Though I don't know what any of the rest of the stuff hooked on is."

"I know—I've been inside the plant Bob's father had." She lifted an inquiring eyebrow at him and went on as he nodded. "The pipes are the exhaust gases, all right, and those big square things are the motors and fans—they put in one at each five hundred feet or less

| 167 |

of piping. The things they're wrapping around the pipe must be the heaters to keep the gases hot. Are they going to try to suck all that out?"

Doc didn't know, though it was the only thing he could see. But he wondered how they'd get around the problem of moving in close enough to do any good. "I heard your husband order some thermodyne bombs, so they'll probably try to gassify the magma; then they're pumping it down the river."

As he spoke there was a flurry of motion at one side and his eyes swung over instantly, to see one of the cranes laboring with a long framework sticking out from its front, holding up a section of pipe with a nozzle on the end. It tilted precariously, even though heavy bags were piled everwhere to add weight, but an inch at a time it lifted its load and began forcing its way forward, carrying the nozzle out in front and rather high.

Below the main exhaust pipe was another, smaller one. As it drew near the outskirts of the danger zone, a small object ejaculated from the little pipe, hit the ground, and was a sudden blazing inferno of glaring blue-white light, far brighter than it seemed, judging by the effect on the eyes. Doc shielded his, just as someone below put something into his hands.

"Put 'em on. Palmer says the light's actinic."

He heard Brown fussing beside him, then his vision cleared and he looked back through the goggles to see a glowing cloud spring up from the magma, spread out near the ground, narrowing down higher up, until it was sucked into the nozzle above and disappeared. Another bomb slid from the tube and erupted with blazing heat. A sideways glance showed another crane being fitted and a group of men near it wrapping what might have been oiled rags around the small bombs; probably no tubing fitted them exactly and they were padding them so pressure could blow them forward and out. Three more dropped from the tube, one at a time, and the fans roared and groaned, pulling the cloud that rose into the pipe and feeding it down toward the river.

Then the crane inched back out carefully as men uncoupled its piping from the main line, and a second went in to replace it. The heat generated must be too great for the machine to stand steadily without the pipe fusing, Doc decided; though they couldn't have kept a man inside the heavily armored cab for any length of time if the metal had been impervious. Now another crane was ready and went in from another place; the work settled down to a routine of ingoing and outcoming cranes, and men feeding materials in, coupling and uncoupling the pipes and replacing the others who came from the cabs. Doc began to feel like a man at a tennis match, watching the ball without knowing the rules.

Brown must have had the same idea, for she caught Ferrel's arm and indicated a little leather case that came from her handbag. "Doc, do you play chess? We might as well fill our time with that as sit here on edge just watching. It's supposed to be good for nerves."

He seized on it gratefully, without explaining that he'd been city champion three years running; he'd take it easy, watch her game, handicap himself just enough to make it interesting by the deliberate loss of a rook, bishop, or knight, as was needed to even the odds. . . . Suppose they got all the magma out and into the river; how did that solve the problem? It removed it from the plant, but far less than the fifty-mile minimum danger limit.

"Check," Brown announced. He castled, and looked up at the half-dozen cranes that were now operating. "Check! Checkmate!"

He looked back again hastily, then, to see her

queen guarding all possible moves, a bishop checking him. Then his eyes followed down toward her end. "Umm. Did you know you've been in check for the last half-dozen moves? Because I didn't."

She frowned, shook her head, and began setting the men up again. Doc moved out the queen's pawn, looked out at the workers, and then brought out the queen's bishop, to see her take it with her king's pawn. He hadn't watched her move it out, and had counted on her queen's to block his. Things would require more careful watching on this little portable set. The men were moving steadily and there was a growing clear space, but as they went forward the violent action of the thermodyne had pitted the ground, carefully though it had been used, and going became more uncertain. Time was slipping by rapidly now.

"Checkmate!" He found himself in a hole, started to nod; but she caught herself in time. "Sorry, I've been playing my king for a queen. Doctor, let's see if we can play at least one game right."

Before it was half finished, it became obvious that they couldn't. Neither had chess very much on the mind, and the pawns and men did fearful and wonderful things, while the knights were as likely to jump six squares as their normal L. They gave it up, just as one of the cranes lost its precarious balance and toppled forward, dropping the long extended pipe into the bubbling mass below. Tanks were in instantly, hitching on and tugging backward until it came down with a thump as the pipe fused, releasing the extreme forward load. It backed out on its own power, while another went in. The driver, by sheer good luck, hobbled from the cab, waving an armored hand to indicate he was all right. Things settled back to an excited routine again that seemed to go on endlessly, though seconds were dropping off too rapidly, turning into minutes that threatened to be hours far too soon.

"Uh!" Brown had been staring for some time, but her little feet suddenly came down with a bang and she straightened up, her hand to her mouth. "Doctor, I just thought; it won't do any good—all this!"

"Why?" She couldn't know anything; but he felt the faint hopes he had go downward sharply. His nerves were dulled, but still ready to jump at the slightest warning.

"The stuff they were making was a super-heavy —it'll sink as soon as it hits the water, and all pile up right there! It won't float down river!"

Obvious, Ferrel thought; too obvious. Maybe that was why the engineers hadn't thought of it. He started from the plank, just as Palmer stepped up, but the manager's hand on his shoulder forced him back.

"Easy, Doc, it's okay. So they teach women *some* science nowadays, eh, Mrs. Jenkins . . . Sue . . . Dr. Brown, whatever your name is? Don't worry about it, though—the old principle of Brownian movement will keep any colloid suspended, if it's fine enough to be a real colloid. We're sucking it out and keeping it pretty hot until it reaches the water, then it cools off so fast it hasn't time to collect in particles big enough to sink. Some of the dust that floats around in the air is heavier than water, too. I'm joining the bystanders, if you don't mind; the men have everything under control and I can see better here than I could down there, if anything does come up."

Doc's momentary despair reacted to leave him feeling more sure of things than was justified. He pushed over on the plank, making room for Palmer to drop down beside him. "What's to keep it from blowing up anyway, Palmer?"

"Nothing! Got a match?" He sucked in on the cigarette heavily, relaxing as much as he could. "No use trying to fool you, Doc, at this stage of the game. We're gambling and I'd say the odds are even; Jenkins thinks they're ninety to ten in his favor, but he has to think so. What we're hoping is that by lifting it out in a gas, thus breaking it down at once from full concentration to the finest possible form, and letting it settle in the water in colloidal particles, there won't be a concentration at any one place sufficient to set it all off at once. The big problem is making sure we get every bit of it cleaned up here, or there may be enough left to take care of us and the nearby city! At least, since the last change, it's stopped spitting, so all the men have to worry about is burn!"

"How much damage, even if it doesn't go off all at once?"

"Possibly none, beyond raising the radioactive count of the air a little. If you can keep it burning slowly, a million tons of dynamite wouldn't be any worse than the same amount of wood, but a stick going off at once will kill you. Of course, even if it doesn't erupt violently, the stuff in the swamp afterward will be pure death for months, but that won't bother us. Why the dickens didn't Jenkins tell me he wanted to go into atomics? We could have fixed all that for anyone who'd been partly trained by Kellar. It's hard enough to get good men as it is!"

Brown perked up, forgetting the whole trouble beyond them, and went into the story with enthusiasm, including details on how Jenkins had managed to continue his study of atomic theory, while Ferrel only partly listened. He could see the spot of magma growing steadily smaller, but the watch on his wrist went on ticking off the minutes remorselessly, and the time was growing limited. He hadn't realized before how long he'd been sitting here. Now three of the crane nozzles were almost touching, and around them stretched the burned-out ground, with no sign of converter, masonry, or anything else; the heat from the thermodyne had gassified everything, indiscriminately.

"Palmer!" The portable ultrawave set around the manager's neck came to life suddenly. "Hey, Palmer, these blowers are about shot; the pipe's pitting already. We've been doing everything we can to replace them, but that stuff eats faster than we can fix. Can't hold up more'n fifteen minutes more."

"Check, Briggs. Keep 'em going the best you can."

Palmer flipped a switch and looked out toward the tank standing by behind the cranes. "Jenkins, you get that?"

"Yeah. Surprised they held out this long. How much time till deadline?" The boy's voice was completely toneless, neither hope nor nerves showing up, only the complete weariness of a man almost at his limit.

Palmer looked and whistled. "Twelve minutes, according to the minimum estimate Hoke made! How much left?"

"We're just burning around now, trying to make sure there's no pocket left; I hope we've got the whole works, but I'm not promising. Might as well send out all the I-631 you have and we'll boil it down the pipes to clear out any deposits on them. All the old treads and parts that contacted the R gone into the pile?"

"You melted the last, and your cranes haven't touched the stuff directly. Nice pile of money's gone down that pipe—converter, machinery, everything!"

Jenkins made a sound that was expressive of his worry about that. "I'm coming in now and starting the clearing of the pipe. What've you been paying insurance for?"

"At a huge rate, too! But I didn't expect to get proof that we could prevent any danger from Mahler's Isotope, so I figure I got a bargain. Okay, come on in, kid; and if you're interested, and we live through this, you can start sticking an engineering degree after the

| 173 |

M.D. any time you want. Your wife's been giving me your qualifications and I think you've passed the final test, so you're now an atomic engineer, duly graduated from National!"

Brown's breath caught and her eyes seemed to glow, even through the goggles, but Jenkins' voice was flat. "Okay, I expected you to give me the degree, if we don't blow up. But you'll have to see Dr. Ferrel about it; he's got a contract with me for medical practice. Be there shortly."

Nine of the estimated minimum of twelve minutes had ticked by when Jenkins climbed up beside them, mopping off some of the sweat that covered him. Palmer was hugging the watch. More minutes ticked off slowly, while the last sound faded out in the plant and the men stood around, staring down toward the river or the hole that had been Number Four. Silence. Jenkins stirred and grunted.

"Palmer, I meant to tell you where I got the idea. Jorgenson was trying to remind me of it—not raving —only I didn't get it until Doc jiggled my thoughts. It was one of Dad's, the one he told Jorgenson was a last resort, in case the thing they broke up over went haywire. It was the first variable Dad tried. I was twelve, and he insisted water would break it up into all its chains and kill the danger. Only Dad didn't really expect it to work, as he told me later!"

Palmer didn't look up from the watch, but he caught his breath and swore. "Fine time to tell me that!"

"He didn't have your isotopes to heat it up with, either," Jenkins answered mildly. "Suppose you look up from the watch and down the river for a minute!"

As Doc raised his eyes he was aware suddenly of a roar from the men. Over to the south, stretching out in a huge mass, was a cloud of steam that spread upward and out as he watched, and the beginnings of a mighty hissing sound came in. Then Palmer was hugging Jenkins and yelling until Brown could pry him away and replace him.

"Steam from heat—steam, not explosive spray! Three miles or more of river, plus the swamps, Doc!" Palmer was shouting in Ferrel's ear. "All that dispersion, while it cooks slowly from now until the last chain is finished, atom by atom! The *theta* chain broke, unstable, and now there's everything there, too scattered to set itself off! It'll cook the river bed up and dry it, but that's all!"

Doc was still dazed, unsure of how to take the relief. He wanted to lie down and cry or stand up with the men and shout his head off. Instead, he sat loosely, gazing at the cloud. "So I lose the best assistant I ever had! Jenkins, I won't hold you; you're free for whatever Palmer wants."

"Hoke wants him to work on R—he's got a starting point now for digging into that rocket fuel he wants!" Palmer was clapping his hands together slowly, like an excited child watching a steam shovel. "Heck, Doc, pick out anyone you want until your own boy gets out next year. You wanted a chance to work him in here, now you've got it. Right now I'll give you anything you want! This is one time even the Guilden papers won't be able to twist the truth!"

"You might see what you can do about hospitalizing the injured and fixing things up for the men in the tent behind the Infirmary. And I think I'll take Brown in Jenkins' place, with the right to grab him in an emergency until that year's up."

"Done!" Palmer slapped the boy's back, stopping the protest, while Brown winked at him. "Your wife likes working, kid; she told me that herself. Besides, a lot of the women work here where they can keep an eye on their men; my own wife does, usually. Doc, you and these two kids head for home, where I'm going myself. Don't come back until you get good and ready, and don't let anything spoil your sleep this time!"

Doc pulled himself from the truck and started off, with Brown and Jenkins following through the yelling, relief-crazed men. The three were too thoroughly worn out for any exhibition themselves, but they could feel it. Men and guards were piling in from the gates, joining crazily in the exultation. There were even a few cars forcing their way slowly through the milling ranks of people.

One of them was almost at Ferrel's side when the door swung open and a haggard woman began getting out painfully, crying his name. He stopped, staring at her unbelievingly as she limped toward him.

"Emma!"

She caught him to her briefly, then shoved him away, blushing, as she saw Jenkins and Brown watching her. She choked and made motions toward the car, unable to talk. But it didn't matter. Explanations could come later.

He sank behind the wheel of the car, reaching out a hand for one of hers. Life, he decided, wasn't bad after all; and it would be even better, once they were out of the mob and headed for home.

Then he chuckled and climbed out again. "You three get acquainted, will you? If I leave here without making out that order for extra disinfection at the showers, Blake'll swear I'm getting old and feeble-minded. I can't have that!"

Old? Maybe a little tired, but he'd been that before and with luck would be again. He wasn't worried. His nerves were good for twenty years and fifty accidents more, and by that time Blake would be due for a little ribbing himself.

historical note

Nerves was first written as a long novelette for *Astounding Science Fiction,* way back in March, 1942. This was five months before the official establishment of the Manhattan District (or Project), and more than three years before the first atomic bomb was tested.*

The basic idea came from the editor, John W. Campbell, who suggested that an accident in an industrial atomic plant might make a good story, if told from the view of the company doctor.

Even in those days, science-fiction readers took atomic fission very much for granted. Robert A. Heinlein had already written an excellent story about a fission power plant. And we were sure that the government was interested in the development of atomic weapons, as indicated by the secrecy clamped on all atomic research. Atomic power was just around the corner.

This, however, made the development of a story from Campbell's idea somewhat difficult. I couldn't use an atomic power plant, because Heinlein had covered that. And it would be unwise to write about things that the government wanted kept secret.

The only industrial possibility remaining seemed to be the transmuting of useful isotopes. (An isotope is an atom of a single, particular atomic weight. The

---

* If anyone wants to compare the novelette and this final version, the original can be found in *Adventures in Time and Space,* published by Ballantine Books, 1975.

term is more specific than "element," since elements can be made up of a mixture of isotopes; uranium contains several isotopes, of which U-235 and U-238 are the best known.)

But what isotopes could such a plant make profitably? The answer was discouraging. The elements are arranged in a Periodic Table, from hydrogen to uranium, and all possible isotopes can be located there. Most are already either common or so unstable as to be commercially useless. The few left, such as radioactive cobalt, offered little hope of large-scale use.

However, using expensive research machines, scientists had recently created microscopic amounts of elements that were heavier than uranium, such as plutonium and neptunium. But above those, the isotopes became so unstable that some disintegrated almost at once.

Well, in science fiction, facts should be used accurately when possible; but when facts won't work, one hunts for a theory that will transcend the facts. So I conveniently supposed that the instability was limited to a narrow group of such isotopes, and that isotopes of even higher atomic weight might again become stable. This gave me isotopes of whatever nature I wished from I-350 upwards.

With the theory developed, I went ahead creating a story I could write, including the characters, who always interest me most in fiction. And when I wrote it, I didn't go into great technical detail, since I wanted a good story, not a lecture. I gave the isotopic number, for those readers who could understand, and nothing else. (Somehow in copy-editing, I-631 became I-231 in the printed version; that was ridiculous, since 231 is a known atomic weight. But nobody seemed to notice.) I wanted the story to work as a piece of pure suspense fiction.

Apparently, it worked very well. All those who wrote letters to the editor listed *Nerves* as the best story in the issue. Such rare unanimity was highly gratifying.

However, my efforts not to bump into government secrecy restrictions were a total failure. I learned of this years later from a young scientist who worked at Oak Ridge during the war. She was a science-fiction fan, so when the right day of the month rolled around, she went to the library to borrow the latest *Astounding*. She was refused permission to see it. My story had been stamped top secret and her clearance wasn't high enough for her to read it! Of course, she promptly went to the nearest newsstand where the magazine was on sale and bought her copy there.

No book markets existed for science fiction when I wrote the story. But times changed, and eventually Ballantine Books began looking for such novels. My old friend Frederik Pohl began urging me to expand *Nerves* for them. I resisted, since more than a dozen years had passed and I felt doubtful of being able to recapture the feeling of the story. But he kept after me until I agreed. For that, I'm extremely grateful to him.

I didn't exactly expand it. So far as I could, I left original material untouched. But there were many details I had been forced to leave out originally, to keep the story short enough for magazine use. The action should have begun earlier, with an initial accident setting the stage for the later disaster; and the characters of Jorgenson, Palmer and Doc's wife needed to be developed, along with the events affecting them. Also, the political background should have been covered in greater detail. Now I had a chance to restore to the story all the parts that had been in my head all along but had been sacrificed to space considerations. And also I was finally able to give a little of the theory on which everything was based. But happily, it remained essentially the same story.

Now the novel has gone through five printings. In planning a sixth printing, the publisher has kindly permitted me to go over it again. A third of a century has passed since I first wrote the story, and I can look at it far more objectively. So again I've revised it slightly, eliminating inconsistencies, expanding a bit for clarity—but essentially leaving the story as it was always meant to be.

If I were to write the novel today, rather than at the dawn of the atomic age, it would probably be quite different. I would fill it with the very real dangers of misused or stolen plutonium, the unsolved problem of atomic waste disposal—all the problems that developed over the years. Or, since there are enough books on such subjects, I might not write it at all. Certainly, I'd never go in for such fantasy as the postulate of super-heavy artificial isotopes with increasing stability!

Or would I? Back when this novel was still in its second printing, I opened the September 12, 1967, issue of the *New York Times* to find a surprise on page 30. A science article there reported the creation of a super-heavy atom which was amazingly stable. Dr. Albert Ghioroso, of the Lawrence Radiation Laboratory, stated that it should be possible to create a new group of such atoms—and that they might prove to be stable.

In twenty-five years, my wildest speculation about the future had become a serious theory, proposed by a reputable scientist.

So maybe I'll live to meet Jorgenson, Palmer and Hokusai!

—Lester del Rey
October, 1975